Enid Blyton's

SUMMER STORIES

Other series by Enid Blyton, the world's best-loved storyteller

Stories of adventure

The Famous Five
The Famous Five Colour Short Stories
The Secret Stories

Mystery stories

The Secret Seven
The Mystery Stories

Stories about boarding school fun

Malory Towers
St Clare's
The Naughtiest Girl

Other story collections

Enid Blyton's Holiday Stories
Mr Galliano's Circus Story Collection
Fireworks in Fairyland Story Collection

Enid Blyton's

SUMMER STORIES

Hodder
Children's
Books

First published in Great Britain in 2015 by Hodder Children's Books

A Catalogue record for this book is available from the British Library

ISBN 978 1 444 93122 8

Printed and bound in Great Britain by Clays Ltd, St Ives plc

Hodder Children's Books
An imprint of Hachette Children's Group
Part of Hodder and Stoughton
Carmelite House
50 Victoria Embankment
London EC4Y 0DZ
An Hachette UK company

www.hachette.co.uk

Contents

Introduction

Enid Blyton (1897–1968) is one of the world's best-loved storytellers, writing over six hundred books in her lifetime. From the *Famous Five* to the *Magic Faraway Tree*, her characters and their adventures continue to delight children today. Step into a world full of picnics, trips to the seaside and endless summer days.

Here is a selection of some of her best summertime stories.

Enjoy the stories – and your summer holidays!

The Fish That Got Away

The Fish That
Got Away

'Look!' said Stella, suddenly, sitting up straight.
'Look – there's a boy throwing stones at those
seagulls!'

The others uncurled themselves from the warm
sand on the beach and sat up to look. Sure enough,
they saw a big boy throwing stones at a group of
seagulls at the edge of the sea.

'He'll have to be stopped,' said Peter, but he didn't
do anything about it.

'He nearly hit one of them,' said Jean. 'The beast.
Peter, go and stop him.'

But the boy throwing stones was much bigger than

Peter. Peter didn't move. It was John that got up in a hurry and ran yelling down the beach.

John was smaller than Peter, but he had a very loud voice. You should have heard him shouting at the boy.

'Hey you! Stop that! Throwing stones at birds is NOT allowed! STOP THAT!'

And would you believe it, the boy stopped throwing stones at once, and ran off. He saw everyone on the beach sitting up and staring, and he was ashamed and afraid.

'One of those gulls is hurt, I think,' said Jean, and she got up. 'Good old John – he's the smallest of us all, and yet he was the bravest. You're a coward, Peter.'

'Same to you,' said Peter, at once. 'You're my twin, aren't you? Why couldn't you have gone and shouted?'

'Well, I'm a girl,' said Jean. 'It's boys who should do things like that.'

'That's right – make excuses for yourself,' Peter

4

said sulkily. He didn't get up to join Jean as she went down the beach to John. Nor did Stella. But Stella was the most ashamed! Oh, dear – why had she let John go shouting at that boy all by himself? She ought to have gone with him.

John had gone to the seagull. The others had flown off, but this one stood looking rather dazed. It moved away a little as John got up to it, but didn't fly.

'It's just stunned by a stone, I think,' said John, going carefully up to it. 'Look, Jean, its wing is hurt. I wonder if we could take it home and look after it for a day or two till it recovers. It doesn't seem very badly hurt.'

The gull let John pick it up. Jean was afraid of the big bird and wouldn't touch it, but Stella came running down to help.

'You were brave, John,' she said. 'I should have come with you and shouted, too.'

'You needn't worry! I can manage things like that by myself,' said John. 'Anyway, bullies like that boy are always cowards – they run away at once! Help me with this gull, Stella.'

The gull stayed quietly under John's arm till he reached home. Its eyes were half-shut. It seemed quite dazed.

Mother was very sorry to hear all about it. She bathed its wing, and then told John to take the gull into the garden and put it into the shed, so that it could keep quiet till it felt better.

'Leave the door open,' she said. 'Then it will not feel it is a prisoner. It can go out when it wants to.'

Well, just as the children were sitting down to their tea, they heard the sound of a loud seagull cry: 'EE-ew, EE-ew!' Then they heard the flap of wings. They looked up. Standing on the window-ledge was the gull, its eyes wide open now, looking at them.

'Ee-ew,' said the gull, more quietly, and then it spread its great grey wings and flew off into the sky.

'Well! It came to say thank you!' said Stella. 'It's better now. I'm so glad.'

Everyone was glad. When they went out after tea they went down to the rocks to see if they could make out the gull they had helped. But they couldn't.

'They all look so alike when they are in a bunch together,' said Jean. 'First I think it's this one, then I think it's that one – I just can't be sure.'

No gull came flying down to them, as John half hoped. He thought it would be very nice to have a friendly gull walking round them. But all the birds kept together, and not one gull even looked at the four children.

They walked home by the pier. Peter saw a big notice up. He went over to look at it. Then he called the others.

'I say – look! There's a fishing competition on the pier tomorrow – a prize for the biggest and best fish caught – children under twelve. Well, we're all under twelve. Let's go in for it. You just never know, we might be lucky and catch a big fish.'

'Yes – let's,' said Jean, who liked fishing with a line

off the pier. 'I'm sure Mummy will let us.'

Their mother was only too glad to say she would pack up sandwiches and cake, and let them join the competitors in the fishing on the pier. 'Dear me – how wonderful to get rid of you all for a whole day!' she said, with a twinkle in her eye. 'Now I can go and see Granny.'

About twenty children crowded on to the pier the next day, armed with fishing-rods or lines, and plenty of bait. They all went to look at the prizes – first, second, and third.

The first prize was a big book on ships. 'Hope none of us wins that,' said Stella. 'We've got that book already.'

'The second prize is that shrimping net,' said Peter. 'I'd like that. It's a very fine one.'

The third prize was a beach ball, a nice one. But the four children didn't particularly want that, either, because they already had a very nice one themselves.

'We'll have to hope to win the second prize,' said Peter. 'Bags I do!'

'Bags you don't!' said a boy near him, and Peter grinned.

'Hello, Ken – you in for the competition too? I hope we all get some good fish.'

'My dad says we won't,' said Ken, who was a fisherman's son. 'He says the wind's not right today for fishing off the pier. He says we'll be lucky if we even get a good-sized mackerel! We'll only get tiddly little dabs.'

Well, it was great fun going in for the competition. Peter, John, Jean and Stella all chose good positions and let down their baited lines. They had no fishing-rods, but they considered lines were just as good.

The competition began at twelve. Not one of the twenty children had caught a fish by the time it was one o'clock. It was very disappointing.

They called a halt to their fishing while they gathered together and ate sandwiches and cake and talked. Most of the children knew one another, and it was fun.

At two o'clock they all began fishing again. Ken got the first bite. He hauled up his line in glee. Then he gave a shout of disgust. 'A crab! Look at that! Back you go, crab, I don't want you.'

Back went the crab just as Peter gave a shout. He had felt something pulling at his bait. He hauled up the line but it was only a tiny little dab wriggling on the hook. That wouldn't win any prize at all.

It was rather a slow afternoon, because, as Ken's father had said, the wind was not right for fishing off the pier. One or two more dabs were caught, and a peculiar fish that nobody knew the name of. Two more crabs were caught and thrown back.

Then John caught a fish. He felt the sudden big tug at his line and sat up at once. 'I've got one!' he called in excitement. 'And a big one, too. My word, he's pulling!'

He hauled up his line. Everyone waited breathlessly

to see what fish would come swinging and wriggling out of the water.

'It's a cod! My word, quite a big one!' yelled John in delight.

'You'll win the prize!' called the children.

'It's a beauty!' said Ken. 'You are lucky!'

'Isn't he struggling hard?' said Jean. 'I hope the line doesn't break, John.'

It didn't – but just as John was carefully pulling the fish up to the pierside, something happened. The fish gave a sudden strong flap, and somehow or other got off the hook. It fell downwards to the sea with a splash, gave a flick of its tail, and disappeared.

Loud groans came from everyone. The pier-master, hearing all the excitement, came up.

'Hello – anyone caught a real fish at last?' he said.

'It got away,' said John, dolefully. 'It was very big, indeed, Mr Wills. As big as this!' And he stretched out his arms.

'My word, was it?' said Mr Wills. 'Well, well – it's

always the biggest ones that get away, you know. Better luck next time.'

'Bad luck, John,' said Ken. 'You really deserved the prize for that fish. In fact, I think you ought to get it, even though it got away. Nobody will catch a fish half that size!'

They all went on fishing. Ken caught a plaice, the biggest fish yet, though not half as big as the one that had got away. He put it proudly into his basket.

Then somebody caught a small cod, a codling, but it wasn't as big as Ken's plaice.

Ken suddenly gave a groan. 'Look at those gulls – they've settled on the water round the pier, and now they'll get the fish, not us. Blow them!'

The gulls bobbed up and down, and two or three of them dived in for fish. It really was annoying for the children, but, still, it was almost teatime now, and the competition was nearly over.

The pier-master came up again. 'Time!' he said. 'Put your fish into your baskets, please, and come to the scales to weigh them. Anyone with tiny fish needn't bother – I can see one or two good plaice and a codling, anyway.'

'Oh, I do wish I'd caught that fish that got away,' said John, pulling in his line. 'Ah, look – here comes the steamer!'

The gulls all rose up into the air as the steamer approached, sounding its siren. One of the gulls flew over the pier. As it flew over, something fell from its beak right at John's feet, making him jump.

It was a large mackerel! John stared in amazement and then looked up at the gull, which had now flown off. What a lovely big fish! But could he put it in for the competition? He hadn't caught it.

The others crowded round. 'Yes, you put it in,' they said. 'You caught a much bigger one that got away. And anyway, the mackerel has been caught, and given to you by the gull. It's yours!'

'Yes – we'll let you give it in!' said Ken. They all liked John. 'You had a piece of bad luck – now you've got some good luck!'

'No, I shan't put it in,' said John. 'It wouldn't be fair. But thanks all the same.' He went with the others to see the fish weighed. Ken's plaice was the heaviest. Then came the codling, and a large dab. The pier-master suddenly caught sight of John's mackerel.

'Here – wait a minute! There's another big fish here,' he said, and took it out of John's basket. He swung it on to the scales. 'Why, it's second best,' he said. 'You've won second prize, John!'

'No, I haven't really,' said John, and he told the pier-master the story of the gull and how it had dropped the mackerel at his feet.

Stella suddenly interrupted. 'John! John! Do you know, I believe it must have been that gull you saved yesterday – when you made that boy run – the one who was throwing stones! It must have been the very same gull!'

Well, everyone thought the same. 'How extraordinary,' said Ken. 'Well, you'll have to have second prize, John – you deserve it.'

'No, thanks,' said John. 'I didn't catch the fish, as you all know very well.'

'Now, I'm the judge of this competition,' said the pier-master, 'and what I say goes. There shall be two second prizes, exactly the same – one for the mackerel, and one for the codling. I'll get another shrimping net. Is that all right, everyone?'

'YES!' yelled everybody, and John grinned in delight. The pier-master went to his store cupboard and brought out another net. 'Here you are, John,' he said. 'Share it with the gull, if you like – but we all think it's fair to give you a prize!'

Everyone cheered. John went off with Stella, Jean and Peter, glowing with pleasure. Overhead a gull soared, and the four children heard its laughing cry:

'EE-ew, EE-ew, EE-ew!'

'I bet that's our gull,' said Jean. 'He's glad you got the prize. And so am I.'

The children's mother said it couldn't have been

the same gull, it was just a bit of luck that one had let its fish fall near John. I don't know what to think. What do you think? Whatever anyone says, it seems right that the fish should have gone to John, doesn't it?

The Enchanted Toadstool

The Enchanted
Toadstool

One day Daisy and Jack went for a picnic in Cuckoo Wood. They had their lunch in their pockets, and they wanted to find a nice cool place to eat in, for the day was very hot.

'Look at that little path,' said Jack, pointing to a narrow winding way that left the main path and ran between the trees. 'Shall we go down here, Daisy?'

'It's only a rabbit path, isn't it?' said Daisy. 'We shan't get lost, shall we?'

'Oh, no!' said Jack. 'This is only a small wood, you know. Come on.'

So off they went down the winding rabbit path.

They hadn't gone far before they saw a very curious sight.

'Did you see that?' asked Jack, in excitement. 'That rabbit, Daisy! It had a pair of spectacles on its nose and it carried a bag under its arm.'

'Yes!' said Daisy, with her eyes open very wide. 'I did see it, Jack. Fancy that! Could we really have seen it, do you think?'

'We must have, if we both think we did,' said Jack. 'Oh, Daisy! Do let's go the way he went, and see if we can see him again!'

Off they ran, taking the same path as the rabbit. It wound between the trees, which got thicker and thicker.

'It must lead to the very middle of the wood,' said Jack. 'Isn't it dark here, Daisy? The sun can hardly get between the branches!'

'You're sure we shan't get lost, Jack?' said Daisy, nervously. 'It would be awful if we couldn't find our way back.'

'Look! there's the rabbit again!' said Jack.

Sure enough, there he was, hurrying along in front of them. The children ran faster.

Suddenly they came out into a round clear space, with oak-trees all around in a ring. In the very middle was a large toadstool with red spots. The rabbit sat on this, called out something in a loud voice, and then, hey presto, the toadstool sank swiftly down into the earth and disappeared, taking the rabbit with it!

'Good gracious!' said Daisy, startled. 'Just look at that, Jack! Where has he gone?'

'Into the earth!' said Jack, astonished. 'Come and see!'

They ran to the place where the rabbit and the toadstool had disappeared, and looked at it carefully. There was no sign of anything at all. The grass grew there exactly as it grew all round.

Then suddenly the toadstool came back! It shot up out of the earth just as if it was growing very fast, and caught Jack under the chin. Over he went and over and over, for the toadstool gave him quite a blow. Daisy ran to him and asked him if he was hurt.

'No,' said Jack, rubbing his chin. 'Only surprised, that's all! Fancy it coming back like that, Daisy! And without the rabbit too! Where has he gone, I wonder?'

'I don't know,' said Daisy. 'Isn't it funny, Jack! It's like a story in a book.'

The children went to the toadstool again and looked at it.

'Did you hear what the rabbit said when he sat on it?' asked Daisy.

'It sounded something like "Hi-tiddley-hi-toe, down we go to the land below".' said Jack.

'Let's sit on it for a moment!' said Daisy. 'It would be so exciting! But don't you say what the rabbit said, because I don't want to go down into the earth like that!'

Jack sat on the toadstool. He was just making room for Daisy, when a loud voice cried out:

'Hi-tiddley-hi-toe, down you go to the land below!'

And then, oh dear me! The toadstool shot downwards, taking Jack with it! Daisy was left standing alone, her eyes and mouth wide open with fright.

'He's gone!' said the voice again, and Daisy looked round to see a grinning gnome, who thought he had played a fine trick on Jack.

'What did you do that for?' said Daisy, too angry to wonder at the sight of a gnome. 'Make the toadstool come back again with Jack on it.'

'Can't be done!' said the gnome, with a chuckle. 'Why don't you sit on it and go down too?'

'I'm afraid,' said Daisy. 'Oh, you horrid little gnome, you'd no right to send the toadstool down like that!'

'Why not?' asked the gnome. 'It's my toadstool! Your brother shouldn't have sat on it without asking my permission!'

'Well, we saw a rabbit sitting on it,' said Daisy.

'He's my servant,' said the gnome. 'He's gone to take a message for me to my cousin the Blue Goblin.

He's allowed to use my toadstool whenever he likes.'

'Will the Blue Goblin send Jack back safely?' asked Daisy.

'I don't know,' said the gnome.

'Then as soon as the toadstool comes back I shall go and find out!' said Daisy. As she spoke the toadstool suddenly reappeared, and she ran to it. She sat down on it and called out, 'Hi-tiddley-hi-toe, down we go to the land below!'

In a flash she felt the toadstool sinking swiftly into the ground, and she clutched at the sides. Down it went and down and down. Then *bump*! It came to a standstill and Daisy was shot off.

She stood up and found herself in a round room, very small and lit only by a glow-worm in a glass lamp. The toadstool suddenly shot upwards again, and made Daisy jump. She looked all round for her brother, but she could see him nowhere in the little room. There was no one, and nothing there except the tiny lamp.

'Where's the door?' thought Daisy. She felt all round the room, and at first could find no way of getting out at all. Then she suddenly came to a tiny knob about three feet up the wall. She pressed it, and an opening came, just big enough for her to slip through.

On the other side was a passage, lit by more glow-worm lamps. She made her way down it, and at last came to three turnstiles, each standing at the entrance to three passages. She stood outside them, and wondered which Jack had gone through.

She could see no one to ask for advice, so she pushed through the middle turnstile and ran on down the passage. It led to a yellow door, and she knocked on it.

'Come in, come in, come in!' called a voice. Daisy opened the door and went through. She found herself in a cellar, and saw a flight of stone steps leading up to an open trapdoor. She went up them, and saw a small room in which a brownie sat. He had a very long beard and a long nose. He was writing quickly in a big book, with a large quill pen.

He looked up as Daisy stepped into the room, but didn't seem at all surprised to see her.

'Please, could you tell me where my brother Jack is?' asked Daisy.

'He hasn't been through here,' said the brownie, dipping his pen carefully in the ink. 'He probably went through one of the other turnstiles.'

'Oh dear!' said Daisy in dismay. 'Have I got to go right back through that dark passage again?'

'Not unless you want to,' said the brownie. 'I can find out where your brother is in no time, if you will pay me one penny.'

'Here's a penny Daddy gave me last Saturday,' said Daisy, and she gave him a nice bright penny. He put it in his pocket, and then picked up a large mirror.

'Come here,' he said to Daisy. 'Look into this mirror and think of your brother.'

Daisy looked into the mirror, and to her great surprise she could not see herself at all. She thought of Jack, and there came a picture into the mirror of a little boy sitting on a chair, peeling potatoes, while a rabbit with spectacles on his nose was watching him.

'Oh, there's Jack, and there's that rabbit we saw!' cried Daisy. 'But I don't know now where Jack really is, Mr Brownie. Do you?'

The brownie put on a pair of blue spectacles and peered into the magic mirror.

'Yes,' he said at last. 'He's in the kitchen of the Blue Goblin, and I'm afraid he's a prisoner. That rabbit led him there.'

Daisy began to cry, and this upset the brownie very much.

'Don't do that,' he begged. 'I can't bear it. I'll help you all I can.'

'How can I save Jack from being a prisoner?' asked Daisy, still crying.

'I don't know,' said the brownie, pulling at his long beard. 'I never heard of anyone escaping from the Blue Goblin.'

'Can't anyone save him?' asked Daisy.

'Well, there's the Dumpy Wizard, who's very kind and very clever,' said the brownie. 'He might be able to tell you how to rescue Jack. He lives on Blowaway Hill, a good way from here. You could go and ask him.'

'Thank you very much,' said Daisy, drying her eyes. 'Which way shall I go?'

The brownie took her to his door, and pointed out a steep hill in the distance.

'Do you see that castle?' he asked. 'Well, that's where the Dumpy Wizard lives. But it's very, very difficult to see him, so people say.'

Daisy thanked the brownie and started off in the direction of the castle. She went along a lane whose hedges were starred with the loveliest flowers she had ever seen. She met fairy folk of all kinds, and they seemed just as surprised to see her as she was to see them. She asked her way several times, and at last she seemed to be getting nearer to the hill.

Soon she came to a stile and climbed over it. On the other side was a small elf, crying bitterly, and Daisy stopped to ask what was the matter.

'Look!' said the elf. 'I've broken my lovely new necklace! All the beads have rolled here, there and everywhere! I can't find them because I have left my glasses at home, and I can't see very well without them.'

'I'll find them for you,' said Daisy. She went down on her hands and knees and looked for the beads. They were very small, but Daisy had sharp eyes, and soon she had quite a lot to give the little elf. He counted them, and thanked her very much.

'There are only three missing now,' he said. 'It is so kind of you to have helped me. I've got three extra beads at home, so don't bother to look any more. Where are you going?'

'To Wizard Dumpy's castle,' said Daisy. 'I'm going to ask his help for something.'

'Then you may find this useful,' said the elf, and

pushed something into Daisy's hand. She looked at it and found that it was a tiny key. She was just going to ask the elf what it was for when she saw that he had vanished. She went on her way towards the hill, wondering how she could find such a tiny little key at all useful.

At last she came to the hill. It was very, very steep indeed. A narrow little path led up to it and Daisy started to climb it. Soon she noticed a pixie in front of her, carrying a heavy basket. She caught her up and asked if she could help her.

'I'm very strong,' said Daisy. 'Do let me help you. I could take one side of the basket.'

'Thank you,' said the pixie, surprised and pleased. 'Where are you going?'

'To the castle,' said Daisy. 'I want to ask the wizard's help.'

'He's very difficult to see,' said the pixie, giving Daisy one side of the basket to carry. 'People say that he is quite impossible to get at, so there isn't much hope for you.'

Daisy sighed. It would be dreadful to come all this way and not be able to get help at the end.

'Are you going to the castle?' she asked the pixie.

'No,' said she. 'I'm going to my cottage just near by. Won't you come in and have a cup of tea with me?'

'I mustn't, thank you,' said Daisy. 'I really must see the wizard as soon as I can.'

Just then they arrived at the pixie's cottage. She took the basket from Daisy, and thanked her very much for her kind help.

'Here's something to take with you,' she said, running into her house. 'You may find it useful.'

Daisy wondered whether she was going to be given another key but to her surprise the pixie gave her a little stool!

Daisy tucked it under her arm and said thank you, though she would really much rather not have had it to carry. Off she went again up the hill. The castle seemed very near now.

As Daisy climbed up the steep path, she suddenly felt very hungry. She remembered that she had a packet of sandwiches in her pocket and she stopped to get them out. She found them and took the paper off. How good the sandwiches smelled!

She sat down to eat them. Just as she was beginning, an old woman, rather like a witch, came down the hill. When she saw Daisy she stopped.

'Spare me a little of your lunch!' she begged. 'I am so hungry. I haven't a penny in the world, and if you don't let me share your meal, I shall get nothing all day long.'

Daisy looked at her. She certainly seemed thin and poor. Her shawl was torn and her shoes were in holes. She carried a very long stick with a crook at the end, much taller than herself.

'Here you are,' said Daisy, dividing her sandwiches in half. 'Here are three for you, old woman. And wait a minute! I believe I've got a bar of chocolate here. You can have half of that too.'

The old woman sat down by Daisy, and ate hungrily.

'Where are you going?' she asked.

'To see the wizard in the castle,' said Daisy.

'But you'll never do that!' said the old woman. 'He won't see anyone, you know!'

'Oh dear!' said Daisy, nearly crying. 'Everyone tells me that. I do so hope he will see me!'

The old woman said nothing more until she had finished her sandwiches. Then she rose to her feet, and spoke to Daisy again.

'Thank you very much for your kindness,' she said. 'I haven't anything much to give you in return, but please take this stick. You may find it useful.'

Daisy took the very long stick, wondering how she could ever find such a thing useful. She thanked the old woman and once more went up the hill. Soon she came to the castle gate, and as it was open she went through it.

There were about a hundred steps leading up to the

castle door, and Daisy climbed them all, being very much out of breath when she came to the top. She knocked on the door with the great knocker there, and a small gnome opened it.

'Please can I see the wizard?' asked Daisy politely.

'You can't,' said the gnome. 'He's shut up in his tower and no one can get to him.'

'Oh, please do let me see him!' said Daisy.

'But I tell you, you can't,' said the gnome. 'Not even his servants can get to see him today. He's writing a lot of learned spells, and can't be interrupted unless it's for anything tremendously important.'

'Well, what I've got to ask him *is* tremendously important,' said Daisy. 'Please, please, do tell him.'

'Now look here,' said the gnome, impatiently, 'I tell you I can't tell him. Come in and I'll show you why.'

Daisy followed the gnome into the hall, and into a large room on the right hand side. At the end was a small door with a pane of glass let into it.

'Look through that pane,' said the gnome. 'Do you

see a loop of rope up in the far corner?'

'Yes,' said Daisy.

'Well,' said the gnome. 'When that rope is pulled it rings a bell very loudly in the wizard's tower. Then he leaves his work and comes to see his visitor.'

'Well, why can't you pull the rope?' asked Daisy.

'For lots of reasons,' said the gnome. 'For one thing the door is locked! For another thing I can't reach the rope! Now don't be impatient, little girl. Just sit down quietly in this chair and wait until the wizard finishes his work. He may take all day or he may take a week, I can't tell you.'

Daisy was in despair. She sat down on the chair and thought of poor Jack. She looked round to tell the gnome that she couldn't stay, she would have to go and see the Blue Goblin, when she saw that he had gone. She was alone.

She waited for a little while, and then she felt the tears trickling down her face. She put her hand in her pocket to get out her handkerchief and there she felt the little key that the elf had given her.

She took it out and looked at it. It was very tiny. Suddenly an idea came to her. She jumped up and ran to the little door through which she had seen the rope. She fitted the key into the lock and turned it.

It was the very key for the door! It swung open and, quickly picking up her stool and long stick, Daisy went through, carefully shutting the door behind her in case the little gnome came back and was angry with her.

She looked up at the rope in the corner. It was far too high for her to reach. She suddenly wondered if the long stick that the old woman had given her would reach it. She tried – but alas, it was a little too short. Try as she would Daisy couldn't get the crook handle of the stick into the loop of the rope. Then suddenly she gave a cry of joy.

'My stool!' she shouted. 'If I stand on the stool that the pixie gave me, I may be able to reach it!'

She put it under the rope, and stood on it. Then she

reached up with her stick – and, hey presto, she could just slip the crook handle into the loop! She did so, and pulled hard at the rope.

There came a tremendous noise of ringing bells, so loud that Daisy was almost deafened. Then came the sound of running footsteps and the little gnome burst angrily into the room.

'How dare you, how dare you!' he cried. 'My master will turn you into an earwig for disturbing him!'

'Silence!' a deep voice cried suddenly, and Daisy and the gnome turned to the door. The Dumpy Wizard himself stood there. He was round and fat, not much bigger than Daisy herself, but very, very wise-looking.

'Who rang that bell?' he asked.

'I did,' said Daisy, bravely. 'I wanted to ask your help.'

'How did you get the key to open this door?' asked the wizard, 'and the long stick?'

Daisy told him, and when she had finished he

smiled very kindly.

'Ah, I can see you have been doing some kind deeds,' he said, 'so I cannot refuse to help you. What do you want me to do?'

'Please, could you rescue my brother Jack?' begged Daisy. 'The Blue Goblin has got him as a servant.'

'Certainly,' said the wizard. Then he turned to his astonished servant. 'Fetch my carriage,' he ordered.

In a minute or two a grand carriage, pulled by seven white horses, was at the door. The Dumpy Wizard and Daisy stepped into it, and they drove off. After about half an hour they drew up at another castle, and the wizard thumped loudly at the door.

A goblin, who was dressed all in blue, answered it.

'Where's that boy you've got?' demanded the wizard.

'You must be mistaken, your highness!' said the goblin, trembling. 'I have no boy!'

'WHERE'S THAT BOY YOU'VE GOT?' said the wizard in a very frightening voice.

The goblin said no more. He disappeared into his castle, and came back again with – who do you think? – Yes, Jack! How glad Daisy was! She leaped out of the carriage and ran to meet him. They hugged one another and cried for joy.

The Blue Goblin vanished into his castle and banged the door. The Dumpy Wizard put both his arms round the two children and laughed and cried with them, he was so pleased to see two people so happy.

'You should be proud of your sister,' he said to Jack. 'She has been very brave. Now would you like me to drive you home?'

'Oh, please do!' said Daisy. So they all climbed into the carriage again, and off went the seven horses at a spanking rate. And in ten minutes they were driving down the village street where Daisy and Jack lived! What a stir there was in the little place! Everyone turned out to see them!

They said goodbye to the Dumpy Wizard and he

drove off again. Then they ran indoors to tell their mother all their wonderful adventures. She was just as excited as they were.

'Tomorrow you shall take me into the woods to see that enchanted toadstool!' she said. 'And I'll just tell that gnome what a wicked creature he is for letting his rabbit take Jack to the Blue Goblin.'

But do you know, when they got to the little round clearing, there was no toadstool there at all! They couldn't see the gnome either, so they thought he must have gone away in case someone should come and scold him for what he had done. All they saw was a solemn grey rabbit peering at them from behind a bush.

'Is that the rabbit who took you away, Jack?' cried Daisy – but before they could see for certain, he was gone! Still, I shouldn't be surprised if he was the rabbit, would you?

Jimmy and the Elephant Man

Jimmy and the Elephant Man

Jimmy wanted to go to the circus. All his friends were going – but somehow his parents couldn't be bothered to take him. His mother wasn't very well and his father seemed very busy.

'I don't like to bother them,' thought Jimmy. 'They will only get cross with me. But how I wish I could go!'

'Jimmy! Jimmy! I want you to run an errand for me!' called Mother. 'Hurry, now! Go to Mrs Brown and tell her I need twelve new-laid eggs tomorrow.'

Jimmy put down his book and ran off. He went down the street, up the lane, over the hill, down to the farm, and all the way back again. It was a long walk, and Jimmy felt quite tired by the time he reached his own street once more.

Just as he turned into his street he saw an old lady sitting on a doorstep, crying! This was such a surprising sight that Jimmy stood still and stared for a moment, quite forgetting that it isn't kind to stare. But he didn't think that grown-ups ever cried.

'What's the matter?' he said to the old lady, going up to her. 'Don't you feel well?'

'I've lost my purse with all my money in it,' said the old woman, wiping her eyes with a big white handkerchief. 'And there's my son's watch in it, too, which has just been mended. He will be so cross with me!'

'Where do you think you lost your purse?' asked Jimmy, looking all round as if he expected to see it in the road somewhere.

'I've just come back from Mrs Brown at the farm,' said the old lady. 'I must have dropped it somewhere on the way.'

'How funny!' said Jimmy. 'I've just been to Mrs Brown's too – but I didn't see your purse on the way back. Of course, I was running, and not looking.'

'I suppose you wouldn't go back and see if you can find it for me, little boy?' asked the old lady.

Jimmy didn't want to at all. He had already been all the way there and back, and he was tired and wanted to sit down with his book. It would be horrid to have to go to the farm again. But the old lady looked very sad, and he didn't like to think of someone as old as his granny sitting on a doorstep and crying like that.

'I'll go and find it for you,' he said. 'You go home and sit down. I'll bring you the purse if I find it. Where do you live?'

'Number six, in the next street,' said the old lady, getting up. 'Thank you kindly, little boy.'

She walked slowly down the street, and Jimmy went back down the lane, looking everywhere for the purse. He kicked up the leaves, he looked under the hedges – but he couldn't find that purse anywhere in the lane. He went up the hill and looked there. He went almost to the farm, hunting all the way – and just as he got to the first farm gate he saw the purse! It was a big brown one, lying in the mud! How pleased Jimmy was to see it!

He picked it up and ran off at once. His legs were really very tired by this time, but he felt so pleased about the purse that he didn't think of that!

He went to number six in the street next to his and knocked.

'Come in!' cried a voice. Jimmy went in. The old lady was sitting down by a bright fire, drinking a cup of cocoa.

'I've found your purse!' said Jimmy, and he put it into her lap. 'Wasn't that lucky!'

The old woman picked it up and opened it. She nodded her head. 'Yes,' she said, 'all my money's there – and my son's watch too. Now, little boy, would you be so kind as to take this watch to my son for me? I'm too tired to go out again, and he wants it tonight.'

Well, Jimmy thought that was too bad! To go out again! But never mind, he'd do it! He took the watch from the old lady, asked her where he was to take it and went out. Before he did anything more he ran home to tell his mother what had happened to him. She was getting quite worried about him.

'Well, Jimmy, you've been very kind to the old lady,' she said. 'Did she give you a reward to show she was grateful?'

'No, Mum,' said Jimmy. 'I expect she couldn't afford to give me anything – and anyway, I didn't want anything. I didn't like to see her crying.'

He went off with the watch. He had to take it to a house not very far away. He knocked at the door and asked for Mr Siglio. That was the name of the old lady's son.

'He's upstairs,' said the woman who opened the door. 'You'll just catch him. He's off to his elephants in a minute!'

'His elephants!' said Jimmy, in surprise. 'What do you mean?'

'Oh, he's the man that makes the elephants do their tricks at the circus,' said the woman. 'Didn't you know? Yes, he has eight fine elephants, and they all love him as if he were their brother! You should see how they twine their trunks round him and fuss him! Ah, you can see that man's been kind to his beasts!'

Mr Siglio sounded rather a nice man, Jimmy thought. He went up the stairs and knocked on another door. He went in and there was the famous Mr Siglio, dressing himself up in yellow trousers, a bright blue coat, and a great blue top hat, just as he appeared in the circus posters which were all over the town.

'Hello, hello!' said Mr Siglio, looking at Jimmy. 'And who have we here? Mr Tickle-me-up – or Master Tumble-me-down?'

'No,' said Jimmy. 'My name's Jimmy, and I've brought you your watch. I saw your mother sitting on a doorstep and crying because she had lost her purse with her money in it and your watch too. I was lucky enough to find her purse and she asked me to bring you the watch. So here it is!'

'And very kind of you too,' said Mr Siglio, taking the watch and stuffing it into his trousers pocket. 'What can I do for you in return?'

'Oh, nothing, thank you,' said Jimmy. 'I hope your elephants perform well tonight.'

'Have you seen them at the circus?' asked Mr Siglio.

'No,' said Jimmy. 'I haven't been, and I'm afraid I'm not going either.'

'Bless us all!' said Mr Siglio, putting his blue top hat on his head, all on one side. 'Here's a boy who hasn't seen my famous elephants! I can't allow this! Run home, boy, and tell your mother that Mr Siglio, the famous elephant man, wants you to help him at the circus tonight!'

So that night Jimmy went to the circus – and will you believe it, Mr Siglio got him into the big ring and made him help with the elephants. Yes, you could have seen Jimmy riding on one – and throwing a ball to another – and giving a bun to a third! He had never had such an exciting time in his life!

'I didn't know that old lady's son was Mr Siglio, the famous elephant man,' he told his father that night.

'Ah!' said his father, 'there's a lot we don't know, Jimmy, till we give a bit of help to somebody. It's wonderful the things that happen then!'

The Little Button Elves

The Little
Button Elves

One-Button, Two-Button, Three-Button, Four-Button and Five-Button were five little elves who were so alike that no one could tell which was which.

Because of this, one of them wore only one button on his tunic, the next had two buttons, and so on – and everyone called them by the number of their buttons.

'Here comes One-Button!' the pixie-folk used to cry as they saw the elf with one button coming down the road.

'Two-Button is out shopping,' they said when they saw the elf with two buttons going out with a basket.

It was quite easy to tell which was which by counting the buttons.

Now one day all five elves went out together to picnic on Bumblebee Common. One-Button carried the kettle, Two-Button carried the bread and butter, Three-Button carried the cakes, Four-Button carried the apples and Five-Button carried the cups and plates.

Just as they were crossing over the little bridge that leads to the common, Three-Button stumbled and fell. He only just managed not to fall into the water beneath – but alas, the cakes did!

How upset all the Button-Elves were! It was dreadful to have no cakes at a picnic tea. Three-Button was very sorry about it, but it couldn't be helped.

They found a nice place to have their picnic and then Three-Button said that, as he had lost the cakes, he would take the job of going to ask for water for their kettle. So off he started. He saw a cottage in the distance and walked towards it. As he drew near to it, he smelt a delicious smell of newly made cakes.

He knocked on the door and an old dame opened it.

Three-Button thought that she looked very like a witch, but she had kind eyes so he felt sure that she couldn't be.

'Please may I have some water for my kettle?' he asked. 'Certainly,' said the old dame. 'Step into my kitchen and take some from the tap.'

So Three-Button walked into the kitchen and filled his kettle.

Then he suddenly caught sight of the table and his eyes and mouth opened in surprise – for it was piled high with hundreds of cakes, all newly-made and smelling simply delicious!

Three-Button remembered how he had dropped the picnic cakes into the water and a very naughty thought came into his head. Surely the old dame would never miss five cakes from such a big pile.

In a trice the naughty little elf snatched five buns

from the table, took up his kettle, and ran out of the door.

He raced back to the others and showed them what he had got – but he didn't tell them that he had stolen the buns.

They were very pleased.

Soon the kettle was boiling away merrily and One-Button made the tea. Then the elves set to work on the bread and butter. When they had finished that, they started on the newly-baked cakes. They were simply delicious!

But just as they were handing one another the apples, a curious thing happened. Each elf began to feel very uncomfortable.

They looked at one another and then cried out in dismay. 'We're all getting very fat!' they cried, and pointed to each other.

Sure enough they were! Their little tunics became very tight, and their toes burst out of their boots. Soon their hats were much too small and fell off their heads.

'What is it?' cried One-Button. 'What can be the matter with us?'

But none of them knew. It was really dreadful. They grew bigger and bigger and at last, with a pop, One-Button's little button flew off his tunic! Then Two-Button's two buttons flew off too, and Three-Button's and Four-Button's.

Five-Button's popped off as well and soon the grass was strewn with all their buttons.

Crying bitterly they ran home. Everyone they met stared at them in astonishment. When they got home, they shut themselves up and looked all through their magic books to find out what was the matter with them.

And very soon they discovered that pimpernel cakes eaten newly-made caused people to grow terribly fat all in a hurry.

Then Three-Button began to sob and he confessed to the others that he had stolen the five cakes he had brought to them. 'I expect they must have been pimpernel cakes,' he wept. 'I remember seeing a lot of pimpernels growing round the old woman's cottage. Oh, whatever are we to do?'

'Wait a minute!' cried One-Button eagerly. 'Here is a page that tells us what to do to get back to our own size again. Listen: Melt salt and sugar together in a silver thimble and drink it in front of a fire. Then you will grow thin once more!'

It wasn't long before all the elves were solemnly drinking salt and sugar from silver thimbles in front of their kitchen fire.

No sooner had they finished than they suddenly shrank back to their ordinary size! How glad they were! They took hands and danced round and round in glee.

Just then a pixie friend of theirs came in to see them.

'Oh,' he said, 'I just wanted to know if Two-Button would – but, dear me, which of you *is* Two-Button? You haven't any buttons on at all and you're so alike that I can't possibly tell which is which!'

The Button-Elves looked at each other.

Of course, the Buttons had popped off their tunics when they had grown so fat – and now no one would know which was which! And to make things much worse, the elves themselves couldn't remember who had one button, and who had two, three, four and five.

'*Now* what are we to do?' asked the elves in despair. 'Who can tell us who is who?' All the little folk of the town came to try and help them but, really, the elves were so much alike that it wasn't a bit of use.

'There is only one person who could help you and that is Dame Pimpernel up on Bumblebee Common,' said a pixie. 'She is a very clever person indeed.'

'That must be the old woman whose cakes we took,' said one of the Button-Elves. 'Well, we'd better go and confess, and perhaps she will help us.'

So off they all went and soon arrived at Dame Pimpernel's cottage.

She was very much surprised to see them, and even more astonished when she heard that they had stolen five of her cakes and had grown so fat.

When she heard that all their buttons had popped off, she laughed till the tears ran down her wrinkled cheeks.

'Please don't laugh at us,' begged the Elves. 'We have managed to get thin again but, you see, we don't know which of us is which now. People say that you are clever and can tell us.'

'I can tell you easily enough,' said old Dame Pimpernel. 'But you must do something for me in return. You have certainly been punished for the naughtiness of one of you but I think you should be punished a little more. The next time you will all remember not to touch things belonging to other people.'

'What shall we do for you, then?' asked the Button-Elves humbly.

'You can come and feed my chickens for me every day,' said the old woman. 'I really haven't time.'

'Very well, we will take it in turns to come every

day,' promised the elves. 'Now do please tell us which is which.'

'Well, One-Button's button has gone, but his one button-hole has not!' said the dame with a laugh, and she hooked her finger into One-Button's one button-hole. 'You are One-Button. Two-Button is the one with two button-holes, of course, and Three-Button the one with three. Four Button and Five-Button can easily find themselves by counting *their* button-holes too. What a lot of little sillies you are! You could easily have thought of that for yourselves.'

Then the Button-Elves began to laugh. 'Ha-ha!' they went. 'He-he! Ho-ho! What sillies we are! Thank you, Dame Pimpernel; now we will go home and sew on our buttons again. Tomorrow One-Button will come and feed your chickens for you!'

Off they ran and got out their needles and thread. They sewed on their buttons and then felt very happy, for once again they knew which of them was which.

Each day they take it in turns to feed Dame

Pimpernel's chickens. On baking-day they smell the newly-made cakes and see them on the kitchen table – but you may be sure that not one of the Button-Elves goes near them!

The Girl Who
Was Left Behind

The Girl Who Was Left Behind

'Tomorrow we're going for a day by the sea, by the sea!' sang the children in Miss Williams's class.

'Well, mind you are none of you late for the coach,' said Miss Williams, gathering up her books. 'The coach will be at the Town Hall at ten o'clock. It will wait for ten minutes only, then it will start. So you must all be very punctual!'

'We'll be there before the bus!' said Millie.

'We'll be ten minutes early!' cried John.

'I'll have to do my mother's shopping first, but I can get there by ten o'clock,' said Alice.

They all went home, happy because they were to

have a day's holiday by the sea tomorrow. Paddling, bathing, digging – what fun they would have!

All the children were up early the next day. It was Saturday. Most of them had little jobs to do. They had to make their own beds. They had to tidy up their toys. They had to feed chickens, or perhaps help with the shopping.

'I'm off to do my mother's shopping now,' said Alice, peeping over the fence at Millie, who was sitting reading in her garden. 'Wait for me, won't you? I'll be back as soon as I can. Then we'll run together to the Town Hall to get into the coach.'

'I'll wait for you,' promised Millie. 'But don't be late, for goodness' sake!'

Alice set off. There was a lot of shopping to do, and the shops were full. She stood for a long time at the greengrocer's, but at last she was served. Then on she went to the baker's and to the chemist's.

She looked at a clock. Half past nine. She must hurry home now, because she had to put on a clean dress. She would just have enough time.

She hurried home. She gave her mother the shopping and counted out the change. She was a good, sensible little girl, and her mother trusted her with a lot of things.

Then she went upstairs to put on a clean dress. But, oh dear, it had a button missing! Never mind, there was just time to sew it on. Alice got out her needle and cotton.

Soon she heard Millie coming in from next door and calling up the stairs.

'Do come, Alice. It's five to ten! Do come. I shan't wait for you.'

'Coming, coming!' cried Alice, and slipped her dress over her head. She buttoned it quickly, picked up her bag, and ran downstairs. She kissed her mother goodbye, and ran out with Millie.

'It's ten o'clock already,' said Millie. 'The coach will be there. We shan't get the best seats.'

They ran down the street. Just as they got to the

corner a boy came round on a bicycle. A dog ran across the road, and the front wheel of the bicycle ran into him. The dog yelped. The boy fell off his bicycle with a crash, and the bicycle fell on top of him. He lay still, stunned for a moment.

The girls stopped in alarm. Alice ran to the boy. He opened his eyes and sat up, rubbing his knee, which was bruised and bleeding. 'I feel funny,' he said. 'I've hurt my knee. Oh, look at my poor bicycle. I can't ride it home. The front wheel is bent. And all the things have fallen out of my bag. Could you pick them up for me, please?'

He was a boy about Alice's age, but she did not know him. She began to pick up the spilt things. Millie wouldn't help.

'Alice! We simply can't stop! Let someone else help him! We've got to catch that coach!'

'You help me, then, and we'll be able to,' said Alice. 'You pick up the things, and I'll help the boy up. Go on, Millie.'

'What, and miss the coach that is going to take us to the sea!' cried Millie. 'It's five past ten already! I'm going. Are you coming or not, Alice?'

'Oh, yes, yes, just wait a minute. I can't leave this boy till he can stand up properly and wheel his bike,' said Alice, anxiously. 'There's nobody else about to help him. You go on, Millie, and just tell Miss Williams I'll be along in a minute. Don't let the coach go without me.'

Millie ran off, looking cross. How silly of Alice to mess about like that! Let the boy help himself! He wasn't badly hurt. He could easily pick up his own things. Well, even if Alice was going to miss the coach, Millie wasn't!

She tore round the corner and ran down to the Town Hall. Thank goodness, the coach was still there. All the other children were in it. Miss Williams was standing beside it, looking anxiously for Millie and Alice.

'Where's Alice?' she said.

'Oh, she's messing about round the corner!' said Millie, unkindly. 'She just won't be quick. I did tell her we'd be late. I left her behind.'

'The naughty little girl,' said Miss Williams, looking at her watch. 'I'll wait one more minute, and then we shall go.'

Alice helped the boy to his feet. He seemed a bit better. All his things were soon back in his bag. His bicycle could not be ridden so he would have to wheel it home.

'You sit down on that wall over there for a few minutes before you wheel your bike home,' said Alice, 'then you'll feel well enough. I'm sorry I can't stay and see you home, very sorry, but you see, the coach will only wait until ten minutes past ten.'

She ran off and the boy looked after her, thinking what a kind little girl she was. It was nice to find someone kind when you were hurt and dizzy. Kindness was one of the best things in the world.

Alice rushed round the corner and looked anxiously

at the Town Hall, which she could see from there. There was no coach waiting for her! It had gone! Yes, there it was, climbing the hill beyond. It hadn't waited.

Alice stood and looked after it. It hadn't waited. Just because she had stopped to be kind, she had missed a lovely day by the sea. Millie, who hadn't been kind at all, had caught the coach.

'But I couldn't help stopping to help that boy,' said Alice. 'I just couldn't. And now the coach has gone without me.'

Tears came to her eyes and trickled down her cheek. She had hurried so much, she had done all the shopping, she had had plenty of time to get to the coach – and yet she was left behind.

She turned to go home. She had forgotten about the boy sitting on the wall. She did not see him as she walked past him, her tears blinding her. She gave a little sob. She was so dreadfully, dreadfully, disappointed.

The boy saw her in surprise. Hadn't she told him she was going to catch a coach? Surely it hadn't gone without her!

'Hi!' he called. 'What's the matter? Come over here and tell me.'

So Alice told him, and then it was the boy's turn to comfort poor Alice. 'What a shame!' he said. 'I stopped you from catching the coach. Oh, I do feel dreadful about it. Poor, poor Alice.'

'I can go home with you now, and wheel your bicycle, if you like,' said Alice, wiping her eyes. 'You look rather pale, and you ought to have your knee bathed. Come along.'

So she took the boy home, wheeling his bicycle for him. He lived in a lovely house about three streets away. His mother was in the garden, and came running to meet him.

'What have you done, Donald? Oh, your poor knee. What has he done, what happened?'

Alice told her. Then Donald told his mother how

Alice had helped him. She was so grateful.

'Come along in and have some lemonade,' she said. 'I'll just bathe Donald's knee. I don't think it's really very bad.'

While his mother was bathing his knee, Donald told her how poor Alice had missed the coach because she had stayed to help him. 'So there will be no day by the sea for her,' he said. 'And all because of me!'

His mother looked thoughtful. Then she smiled. 'Alice shan't miss her day by the sea!' she said. 'I will take her, and you, too, in the car! It will do you good to have a blow by the sea, after this nasty little fall. We will go to your Auntie Lou's for the day and have a lovely time! Would you like that?'

'Oh, yes!' said Donald, cheering up at once. 'Shall I go and tell Alice? Have you finished with my knee? Oh, won't she be pleased!'

Alice was. She could hardly believe her ears. After her big disappointment it seemed too good to be true that she was going to have a day by the sea after all!

She thanked Donald's mother shyly, and her eyes shone with joy.

They soon set off in Donald's mother's little car. First they went round to Alice's mother and told her. She was very surprised, but pleased to know that Alice had been so kind.

Then off they went. It was a fast little sports car, and Donald's mother drove well. Alice enjoyed it. She had never been in a sports car before, and she thought it was lovely.

'We're going so fast,' she said. 'Do you think we'll pass the coach that the others are in?'

'Well – they had a good start,' said Donald's mother. 'We may get there about the same time.'

The funny thing was, they did! Just as the car drew up on the seafront for the two children to look at the calm blue sea, a big coach drew up too – and it was the one with all the schoolchildren in!

'Look! There's Alice! Surely that's Alice!' Millie cried in amazement. 'Alice, Alice, how did you get here? We left you behind!'

She jumped down and ran to Alice. But Donald did not welcome her. 'This is the other girl who saw me fall,' he said to his mother. 'But she didn't help. She just stood and said they would miss the coach, and ran off without Alice and she didn't even get the coach to wait!'

Millie went red. She knew she had been selfish and unkind. She went back to the others, still red. Now she wished she had been kind, too! Here was Alice, going to have a lovely day with Donald's nice mother – and going back in a sports car! And Millie had thought her so silly to stay behind and help.

Alice had a wonderful day. Donald's Auntie Lou was as kind as his mother, and they all four had a picnic on the beach and ice creams afterwards. They had ice creams again at teatime, and Donald and Alice had three rides each on a donkey, and a lovely bathe.

'Now we must go home,' said Donald's mother, who had been watching Alice and thinking what a well-mannered, nice little girl she was. 'Come along.'

'Oh, I wish the day wasn't over!' said Alice with a sigh. 'I have so loved it.'

'We'll have more days like this,' said Donald's mother. 'You must come to tea with Donald every week. You will be a nice friend for him – someone who is kind and unselfish. Donald is kind, too, so you will make a good pair!'

They do, and they are very happy playing together. 'Your bit of kindness brought you a big reward,' Alice's mother said. It certainly did, but I think Alice deserved it, don't you?

A Story of
Magic Strawberries

A Story of Magic Strawberries

Once upon a time there lived a king called Framboise, who was very, very rich. He loved money. He was very greedy, very mean, and very cunning. His people were made to give him money for this and money for that, until they became very poor, and could afford nothing but the cheapest things to eat and the poorest things to wear.

They did not dare to grumble, for if they did the King told his soldiers to take them to prison, and off they went.

King Framboise was fat, for he loved food. He always dressed himself in the grandest clothes, for though he was mean, he was also vain. He loved to drive through the city in his gold carriage, drawn by twelve white horses, and see all his poor people bowing to him. Then he felt very grand indeed.

'I am a wonderful king,' he thought. 'No other king has as much money as I do, or can dress so finely.'

Now, it happened one day that a stranger came to the country of King Framboise. He was an odd little fellow, dressed in brown and green, with the merriest twinkling eyes you could imagine. He played jolly tunes on a flute, and sounded just like a happy blackbird.

He walked happily up the village street, whistling on his flute, and all the folk peeped out to see him.

'Come out and dance to my music!' he cried, and played a merry jig.

One by one the people came out, but they were so poorly clad, and so thin, that the flute player stared. 'Why do you starve yourselves so?' he cried. 'Surely your fields provide you with food to fatten your cheeks and put dancing into your feet.'

'Our King takes most of our money,' whispered a woman to him. 'And what is left is barely enough to keep ourselves.'

The flute player looked sad as he went to the next village. He stopped and looked at the tumbledown cottages.

'Hey, folk!' he cried. 'Why don't you mend your houses?' And then he played such a merry tune that all the villagers came out to hear.

But he couldn't make them dance. It is only happy people who can dance, and they were some of the saddest people in the whole world.

'We don't have enough money to get our houses mended,' they told him. 'The King takes so much from us, and we dare not refuse him.'

The little man looked sadder still. He spent the night at the village, and heard much more before he set off on his journey again the next day.

Soon he arrived at the King's city. As he was

walking through it, he heard a great trumpeting, and down the street came the King in his golden carriage, looking very splendid, very fat, and very rich.

The flute player stood and stared at him.

'You are vain,' he thought, 'and you are fat and greedy. You are also rich! Now, how can I use these things for the good of your people?'

He went away and thought. Then a smile came over his face, and he chuckled.

He went to a strawberry field, and for two pieces of silver was allowed to pick the biggest strawberries he could see. They were very ripe and very red, and soon the flute player had an enormous basket full of the biggest strawberries that had ever been seen.

Then he put them down in a corner of the field and blew a magic tune over them. And all the time he smiled and smiled.

That afternoon he took the basket of strawberries to the street outside the palace, and walked up and down, crying, 'Strawberries! Strawberries! Juicy and sweet, the finest in the world! Strawberries! Strawberries!'

The King happened to hear him shouting, and went to the window. He saw the basket of delicious strawberries, and his mouth watered. He was very fond of strawberries.

'Ask that fellow how much his strawberries are,' commanded the King.

A footman ran down the street.

'Tell His Majesty that I paid two pieces of gold for them, and I want three, for I had to pick them in the hot sun,' answered the flute player. The footman told the King.

'Much too dear, much too dear!' said His Majesty. 'The fellow is nothing but a cheat. Go down and tell him I will give him one piece of gold, and even that is too much.'

The footman went down and told the flute player.

'I'm sorry,' he said, 'but the strawberries are mine to sell at what price I choose. And three pieces of gold is the price.'

When the King was told this answer, he grew angry. He meant to have the strawberries, but he didn't mean to pay anything like such a high price as three gold pieces for them.

'Tell the fellow to bring them up, and I will pay him,' he said.

So the flute player brought his big basket of strawberries to the King. Footmen set them out on a great gold dish, and put them in front of King Framboise, who began to eat them at once.

You will hardly believe it, but he ate them all, every one!

When he had finished he held out just one single piece of silver to the flute player.

'Here,' he said, 'they are not worth three pieces of gold. They are not even worth one piece of gold. Take this silver piece and be gone.'

'Your Majesty,' said the flute player sternly, 'I want my three pieces of gold!'

The king frowned angrily.

'Soldiers, seize him and put him out!' he cried.

But before the flute player could be seized, he put his flute to his lips and played a strange little tune. Then he laughed, bowed, and ran from the palace.

King Framboise was just going to order his soldiers to go after him, when he felt something creaking inside his head.

He felt very funny. Something strange was happening to his head. Could it be growing bigger? No, things like that don't happen suddenly, thought the King, puzzled and frightened.

Then he looked at his soldiers. They were all staring at him in the greatest surprise and astonishment. Then one by one they turned away from him to hide their smiles.

King Framboise got up and went across to the mirror. What he saw there made him stare with horror and amazement.

His head was shaped just like a big strawberry!

There were his little eyes, his big nose, and his mean mouth, just as usual – but, dear me, they seemed quite lost in his great strawberry-shaped head that sat on his collar as if it were ready to be picked.

'It's magic!' he gasped. 'Those strawberries were magic! Fetch that flute player, quick!'

The soldiers rushed out, laughing, and hunted for the flute player. They soon found him and brought him back, taking care to be very polite, in case he decided to use his magic on them, as well as on the King.

When the King saw him, he roared at him.

'Strawberry seller! What do you mean by this? Do you want to be put in prison for the rest of your life?'

'No,' answered the little man, smiling. 'Ha-ha! Excuse me laughing, but you do look funny! Your people will smile for once, when they see you now!'

'See me! I'll never let them see me like this!' shouted the King. 'Use your magic and make my head become its proper shape!'

'No, no,' said the flute player. 'It is a punishment for you!'

The King almost choked, he was so angry.

'Off with his head!' he cried to the soldiers. 'Off with his head!'

'Remember,' said the flute player, 'whatever you do with my head will not alter yours! I am the only person who can take the spell away, and if you kill me, you will be strawberry-headed for the rest of your life. You will forever be known as King Strawberry Head!'

The King sat silent. It was true. This little flute player was the only one who could undo what he had done. He certainly mustn't kill him!

'Leave me alone to speak with this man,' said the King at last to his soldiers.

They went from the room. The King stared at the little man.

'Here are four gold pieces!' he said. 'That is one more than you asked for. Take them and cure me quickly.'

The little man laughed.

'I want more than that!' he said. 'I want half the gold you have in your treasury.'

The King was too astonished to speak. What did the fellow mean? Was he mad?

'No, I'm not mad!' said the flute player, reading the King's thoughts. 'I want half the gold in your treasury!'

'But, goodness gracious, you don't suppose I'd give you that much, do you?' squealed the King in anger. 'You would completely ruin me!'

'Stuff and nonsense!' answered the flute player. 'You are the richest man in the world, and your people are the poorest folk on earth. You take their money to hoard for yourself, to buy your grand robes and to feed your great appetite. Your people live in hovels and eat little. They do not have any dancing in their feet, nor laughter in their eyes. I'd say you should be ashamed, King Framboise!'

The King grew red all over his great strawberry-shaped face.

'It is not true,' he said.

'But I say it is,' said the little man. 'You big, rich, vain, greedy thing! How everyone will laugh at you!'

The King felt very sorry for himself. Whatever in the world was he to do? He hated the idea of giving so much away to this horrid little strawberry seller.

'Put on your coat, and wrap up your head in my scarf,' said the flute player to King Framboise suddenly. 'I want to take you outside and show you a few things.'

'No, no,' cried the King, 'I won't go out like this!'

'You will!' said the little man – and the King did.

He was taken through the city. The flute player showed him this and that, the thin children and the poorly dressed men and women, the sullen faces and the sad eyes. He heard how the people grumbled about him, and how much he was hated. Nobody knew that this big man with the odd-shaped head was the King.

King Framboise's ears began to burn and he wanted to go away and hide. How awful to be hated like that!

'I didn't know!' he whispered to the flute player. 'I didn't know! I didn't know!'

'No. You were too wrapped up in your selfishness to bother about anything else!' said the little man scornfully.

When they were back at the palace, the flute player looked at the King.

'Well,' he said, 'what about that money? Are you going to give it to me?'

'What would you do with it?' asked the King.

'Give it back to your people!' was the answer. 'It rightfully belongs to them!'

The King sat for a long time without saying anything.

'I ought to do that, not you,' he said at last. 'If I took it from them, it is I who should give it back. I will treat my people better in the future, and perhaps I may win their love.'

Suddenly he stopped speaking and put his hands to his head. Something was happening! Whatever was it?

'Is my head growing larger?' cried the King. 'Oh dear! Oh dear! Oh dear!'

He rushed to the mirror and gazed into it in astonishment. 'Why!' he cried, 'it's all right again! It's the same shape that it was this morning! The spell has been broken!'

'You broke it yourself!' said the flute player, smiling at him. 'I wish you good evening. My work is done!'

And to the astonishment of the King he went gaily dancing from the room, playing on his flute the merriest tune ever heard, and vanished in the darkness outside.

King Framboise sat and felt his head and thought. And the result of his deep thinking was that he took half of all his gold and gave it back to the people. More than that, he promised he would treat them well and rule them kindly, and he kept his word.

He wondered if his soldiers remembered his strawberry-shaped head, but when he asked them, they looked puzzled, and said no, they could remember nothing so strange as that.

Then the King wondered if he had had a dream, and offered a large reward to anyone who would bring him news of a little flute player, dressed in brown and green.

But no one ever did, and the flute player has never been heard of from that day to this. And, though nobody could think why, King Framboise never ate strawberries again – but I expect you could easily guess the reason, couldn't you?

The Marvellous Pink Vase

The Marvellous
Pink Vase

Once upon a time Mr and Mrs Squabble went to a fair. Mr Squabble spent sixpence on hoopla, and tried to throw wooden rings over the things spread out on a table. Mrs Squabble spent threepence, and she was very lucky. One of her rings fell right over a marvellous pink vase.

It was very tall, and had pink roses painted all the way up. Mrs Squabble was simply delighted with it. When the man gave it to her she beamed with joy.

'Isn't it lovely?' she said to Mr Squabble as she carried it home. 'I wonder where I should put it.'

Now Mr Squabble only liked vases when they were

put so high up on a shelf or bookcase that he couldn't knock them over. So he made up his mind that he would say the vase would look fine on the top of the grandfather clock.

When they got home Mrs Squabble put the pink vase down on the table and looked round her parlour. 'Now where shall I put it?' she said. 'It must be some place where every one will see it, because it really is beautiful.'

'Well, my dear, I should put it on the top of the grandfather clock,' said Mr Squabble at once.

'On the top of the clock!' said Mrs Squabble, in surprise. 'What a silly place! You never put anything on top of grandfather clocks.'

'Well, why not?' asked Mr Squabble. 'It would be quite a new place. I should love to see it there. Then, whenever I looked to see the time, which I do quite twenty times a day, I should see the vase. It's a marvellous place.'

'Well, I don't think so,' said Mrs Squabble firmly.

'I shall put it on this little table here, near your armchair.'

Mr Squabble looked on in horror as he watched Mrs Squabble put the vase on a rickety little table near his chair. He knew quite well that the first time he reached out for his pipe he would knock the vase over.

'Now, my dear,' he said, 'that's a foolish place. Only a woman would think of such a silly place.'

'Oh! How dare you say a thing like that!' cried Mrs Squabble. 'Just because I didn't like the top of the grandfather clock!'

'Well, if you don't like that, what about putting the vase safely up there on the shelf, beside the radio?' said Mr Squabble, trying to speak in a nice peaceful voice.

'Really, Squabble, you do think of some stupid places!' said Mrs Squabble. 'Why, every time you turned on the radio the vase might be knocked over.'

'I don't think so,' said Mr Squabble. 'Though if you

turned on the radio when that dreadful woman with the screeching voice sings, the vase might jump right off in alarm.'

'I'll put the vase on the mantelpiece,' said Mrs Squabble. But that didn't suit Mr Squabble at all.

'I shall knock it over when I reach up for the matches,' he said.

'Clumsy person!' said Mrs Squabble.

'Indeed I'm not!' said Mr Squabble. 'Why, I could walk on flowerpots all round the parlour and not fall off once. And that's more than you could do!'

Well, of course, that was quite enough to make Mrs Squabble fetch in twenty flowerpots from the shed and stand them round the parlour.

'All right!' she said. 'Now we'll just see who is clumsy and who is not! You start walking on the flowerpots that side, and I'll start walking on them this side. And whoever falls off first has lost, and the other one can choose where to put the pink vase. And let me tell you this, Squabble – that I shall win without any doubt at all!'

The two of them started to walk on the upturned flowerpots. They did look silly. Round the parlour they went, and round and round, neither of them falling off, for they were being very, very careful.

And then the cat jumped in at the parlour window and made both Mr and Mrs Squabble jump so much that they fell off their flowerpots at the same moment and fell *crash* against the little table.

The pink vase was there. It wobbled – it fell over – it rolled off the table – it tumbled to the floor with a bang – and it smashed into a hundred pieces!

The cat sat in a corner and washed itself. 'Now they'll both know where to put the marvellous pink vase!' the cat purred to itself. 'There's only one place now – and that's the dustbin!'

When Mollie
Missed the Bus

When Mollie
Missed the Bus

Mollie had gone to tea with Peter. It was a lovely, sunny afternoon, so the two children had their tea in the garden. Peter's mother brought out a lovely feast for them – buttered scones with honey, jam sponge and ginger biscuits.

'Oh, Mummy – what a delicious tea you've made for us!' said Peter. 'I wish I could do something for you in return!'

'You can,' said Mother, laughing at him. 'You and Mollie can take butterfly nets after tea and go and catch those tiresome white butterflies that are laying eggs on Daddy's cabbages. The caterpillars will eat up all the leaves if we don't do something about it.'

'Right,' said Peter. 'We'll do that for you.'

So after tea the two children got butterfly nets and went to catch the tiresome butterflies. But they didn't see any butterflies at all at first, so they picked scores of green caterpillars out of the cabbages, instead.

'They've eaten nearly the whole of this cabbage heart away!' said Mollie. 'Oh, look, Peter – there's a butterfly!'

Then others came and soon the children were trying to catch them all in their nets. Suddenly Peter called out, 'I say – look! Here's an enormous one! It's coming your way, Mollie. Catch it!'

It certainly was an enormous one. But when it saw Mollie's net it flew back towards Peter again. *Crash!* He brought his net straight down on it.

'Got it!' he cried. 'Come and see, Mollie.'

They both peered through the netting in which the butterfly was caught firmly. Mollie gave a startled cry.

'It isn't a butterfly! It's – it's – oh, Peter, it can't possibly be a real live pixie, can it?'

'Of course not,' said Peter. 'Fairies aren't real. I don't believe in them. Don't be such a silly, Mollie.'

'But look, Peter – it's got a little face – and golden hair – and hands and feet,' said Mollie, in excitement. 'Goodness – we've caught a fairy! And I've never, ever seen a fairy in my whole life before!'

Peter raised the net carefully and clapped down his hand on the tiny creature inside. There was a squeal.

'Peter, don't do that, don't. You're hurting the poor little thing,' said Mollie. 'Put it down. It is a fairy!'

'Of course I'm a fairy,' said a tiny, high voice. 'I'm Pippy the pixie. Let me go, you're hurting. How dare you catch me in your net!'

'You're not a pixie,' said Peter, still holding tight. 'There are no such things. You're really some strange kind of butterfly, aren't you?'

'You're hurting me! You're squashing my wings. Let me go, I said,' cried the pixie, squealing out again.

'Certainly not,' said Peter. 'I'm going to put you into a matchbox with some holes in and send you up to a museum to find your right name, and . . .'

'No, no, no!' cried the pixie and tears fell down on to Peter's hand. 'I'll die if you put me in a matchbox!' She turned to Mollie. 'Please make him let me go!' she begged her. 'I can hardly breathe, he's squashing me so.'

'Peter – let her go,' said Mollie. 'You're unkind and very silly. Even if you don't believe in fairies, surely you can see one when she's under your nose. If you don't let her go, I'll go and tell your mother – she'll know a fairy when she sees one!'

'I shan't let her go,' said Peter, obstinately, and squeezed the pixie still more tightly. She screamed, and her head drooped forward.

'You're killing her!' cried Mollie, and she gave Peter a good wallop on the back. He was so surprised to think of the gentle Mollie hitting him so hard that he opened his hand – and out flew the pixie!

'Thank you, kind girl!' she called to Mollie. 'Thank you! I'll return your kindness as soon as I possibly can.'

Peter sulked. He didn't know what to say or think. Mollie tried to make up to him for hitting him. She felt very ashamed of that now.

'Let's go down to your lily pond and sail all your boats,' she said at last. Peter cheered up a bit at that. He went to fetch an armful of small boats, and soon they were bobbing merrily over the water.

'Mollie! Don't forget your bus!' called a voice from the house suddenly. 'It will soon be at the corner.'

'Oh dear,' said Mollie, scrambling up, 'I didn't know it was nearly time. I must go, Peter. Mummy said if I missed the bus she wouldn't let me stay up to supper tonight – and Granny's coming this afternoon, so I really must!'

She got her jacket and then ran to the front gate. Peter came with her. But oh dear! There was the bus sailing merrily round the corner, full of passengers!

Mollie had missed it.

She went back into the garden, crying. 'Now Mummy will be really cross,' she said.

A tiny voice called to her, 'What's the matter?'

Mollie looked up. Pippy the pixie was sitting there right beside her, swinging up and down on a honeysuckle twig.

'I wanted to catch that bus,' she said. 'And I missed it. Oh dear – my mother will be so cross with me for not catching it.'

'I'll catch it for you,' said the pixie. 'Where is it?'

'It's gone round the corner. Anyway, you couldn't possibly catch it – and even if you did it wouldn't come back here for me,' said Mollie.

The pixie flew down to the ground and picked up Peter's butterfly net, which was still there. It was very heavy for her to carry, but she managed it.

'I'm off to catch the bus for you,' she said, and flew right over the house!

'Whatever does she mean?' said Mollie, staring.

'Peter, do you still not believe in fairies?'

'I'll believe in them if that pixie brings the bus back for you,' said Peter, grinning. 'But I know she won't. I wonder what she can be thinking of doing with my net?'

Pippy was doing something strange. She flew to the corner of the road and saw the bus far away in the distance. She flew after it, still carrying the net. When she got near to it, she chanted a strange little spell. At once the handle of the net became longer and longer and longer, and the net part grew wider and wider and wider and very, very big.

It reached the bus. It hovered over it! The passengers on the top looked at it and screamed. They began to hurry quickly down the stairs of the bus, calling out in alarm.

The passengers down below were frightened and jumped off, too. The driver and conductor leaped down. What was this strange white thing that was held right over their big bus?

Then *whooosh*! Down came the net and caught the bus! Everyone fled at once.

The net then grew smaller. So did the bus inside. The net turned itself upside down, and held the bus neatly there, both net and bus getting smaller as the handle of the net gradually got shorter and shorter.

At last the pixie could handle it again properly. She flew back to Mollie and Peter with it, looking very pleased.

'I've caught the bus for you,' she said, and neatly tipped it out on the grass. 'There you are – it's nice, isn't it? – Though I really can't think why you want to catch these buses.'

Mollie and Peter stared in astonishment and alarm at the tiny bus. What in the world had happened? It was exactly like the real buses that went up and down the road, but it was very, very small.

'Mollie!' called Peter's mother. 'Did you miss the bus? Silly child! Come here, quickly, because Peter's father has got the car, and he'll run you home.'

Mollie didn't dare to disobey. Clutching the tiny bus in her hand she ran to the front gates where Peter's father was waiting with his car.

'Jump in quickly,' he said. 'I've not got much time.' Off they went. Mollie hadn't a word to say. She was feeling so very, very puzzled. As they went down the road, they came to a crowd of people, talking excitedly together. Peter's father drew up in the car.

'What is it?' he called, and then everyone started talking to him at once.

'It's our bus! It's vanished!'

'A great big thing like a giant net came over it, and we all got out in a hurry, I can tell you!'

'The net caught the bus – and then it seemed to disappear – got so small that we couldn't see where it went.'

'Anyway, it's gone, and hasn't come back – and here we all are, stranded – waiting for the next bus to come along!'

Mollie listened in amazement. Oh dear, oh dear,

it was all because of her that this had happened. That silly little pixie must have thought buses were caught in nets, in exactly the same way that butterflies were. She had gone to catch the bus for Mollie, she had made it shrink – and, at this very moment the little girl was holding the bus in her hand!

She managed to slip out of the car while Peter's father was talking to everyone and no one saw her when she popped the tiny bus down in the gutter and left it there.

'Perhaps if it grows big again everything will be all right,' she thought. 'I'll just take one of the little seat-cushions with me, then I'll know for certain if the bus has grown big, because someone will be surprised when they find out there is a seat-cushion missing and so I shall be sure to hear all about it.'

She slipped back into the car and went off home, very silent.

Peter's father was puzzled and rather scornful of everything the people had told him about the bus.

'All this nonsense about a giant net catching the bus and taking it away!' he said. 'Whatever next?'

But the next day he was even more astonished to hear that the bus had been found again – in the very same place where everyone said it had been caught by the giant net. It was its own size again, of course.

'But there's a seat-cushion missing,' said the conductor to everyone. 'Fancy that! It's too peculiar for words, isn't it?'

It was. Nobody could understand such a mysterious happening. Mollie told her mother all about it, but alas, she didn't believe a word of it!

'Silly girl!' she said to Mollie. 'Making up such a stupid fairytale! You're too old to believe in fairies. Peter doesn't, you know.'

But Peter does! How could he help it when that pixie brought back the bus in his butterfly net? And, of course, Mollie still has the tiny little seat-cushion. She's got it in her own toy bus, and it's her most precious possession.

She showed it to me one afternoon and told me the whole story. That's why I was able to tell it to you, of course!

A Bit of Good Luck

A Bit of Good Luck

'Mary! Have you seen my little gold watch anywhere?' called Granny.

Mary ran indoors to Granny. 'No, I haven't,' she said. 'Oh dear. Have you lost it, Granny?'

'It must have slipped off my wrist when I was weeding in the garden,' said Granny. 'Could you look for it, dear?'

'Yes, of course,' said Mary, and ran out again to hunt for the watch. She looked in all the beds that Granny had weeded. She looked in the tool shed where Granny had gone to fetch flower-pots. She looked in the lettuce bed, because she knew Granny had picked a fat, crisp lettuce for tea.

But the little gold watch was nowhere to be found. What a pity!

'I did love it so much,' said Granny sadly. 'Grandpa gave it to me forty years ago – think of that! It has never once stopped going all those years. Now it will lie out in the cold and rain, and will very soon stop ticking out the time.'

'Oh, Granny, what bad luck!' said Mary. 'You haven't had good luck lately, you know. You broke the red bowl you love so much – and you tore your new dress and spoilt it. I wish I could bring you some good luck!'

'Nobody can do that,' said Granny. 'Well, thank you, dear, for hunting about for my watch. Off you go into the sunshine again. I'll call you when it's dinnertime.'

Mary went out. She was staying a whole week with Granny, and she liked it. Granny was kind and good, and she loved a little joke. Mary *wished* that she could find the treasured little gold watch.

'I wish I could find some good luck for Granny, too,' she thought. 'Oh – I *wonder* if I could find a four-leaved clover? Four-leaved clovers are very, very lucky; there must be magic in them, I suppose. Yes, I think I'll look for one.'

But it wasn't very easy, because Granny's little lawn was so well kept that there were no patches of clover leaves there at all – and hardly even a daisy, but just soft green grass.

'Well, perhaps there will be some clover leaves in the orchard,' thought Mary, and she went to where apple and pear trees stood in the grassy little orchard. She was soon hunting for clover.

'Oh, there's lots here!' she said, in delight, and she began to look through the big clover patches.

She hunted and hunted. Every leaf she found was cut into three! Mary began to get tired of looking carefully at every patch.

Then she suddenly found a four-leaved clover!

Mary was very happy.

'Oh! Here's one at last – in this big, thick patch of leaves. I must have looked at hundreds – and now I've found a four-leaved one!'

Then she found something else! She saw something shining in the very middle of the thick clump of clover. And would you believe it – it was Granny's little gold watch!

'Well! That just *shows* that four-leaved clovers are lucky!' said Mary happily. 'No sooner do I find one than I find the lost watch, too! How pleased Granny will be!'

She ran to the house, holding the watch in one hand and the four-leaved clover in the other. 'Granny! Look what I've got!'

Granny came to the door. 'Oh, Mary! You've found my watch. Where was it?' she cried.

'In the orchard – in the middle of a patch of clover,' said Mary. 'And it's still ticking away, Granny. You just put it to your ear and listen. It didn't mind being dropped. Wasn't it lucky that I found it?'

'It was,' said Granny, putting the watch on her wrist.

'And do you know why I found it?' said Mary. 'I found a four-leaved clover just a minute before – and that's a very lucky thing to find isn't it? It brought me luck at once, because then I found the watch, you see!'

She held out the four-leaved clover to Granny. 'You can have it, Granny darling. You want some good luck, I know, and I'm glad I've got some to give you. You can have the four-leaved clover for yourself.'

'You're a pet,' said Granny, and she took the little four-leaved clover. 'I shall put it my diary and look at it every day. But are you sure you don't want to keep it yourself? Wouldn't you like some good luck?'

'I want *you* to have it,' said Mary. 'I found it for you, really, you know.'

Granny kissed her. 'Well,' she said, 'whatever good

luck comes along while you are staying with me you shall share!'

And believe it or not, that very same day a friend brought Granny an enormous box of chocolates, so Mary had half of them!

The day after that Daddy came to see Granny and Mary, and brought a big slab of ice-cream for Granny. So Mary had to have half of that.

And the third day somebody sent Granny tickets for a Grand Show at the Town Hall – with a Punch and Judy show, puppets and a conjurer!

'One ticket for me – and one for you!' said Granny, giving one to Mary. 'Your four-leaved clover is certainly bringing me luck, Mary!'

'And me, too!' said Mary joyfully. 'I gave my four-leaved clover luck to you, Granny – and *I'm* getting lots of luck too!'

'You deserve it, Mary!' said Granny. And so she did!

The Surprising Buns

The Surprising Buns

Every Saturday Mother Bustle baked some big, curranty buns for her brother, Policeman Plod-Along. He came to tea with her each Saturday afternoon, and curranty buns were his favourite tea-time dish.

He liked them freshly baked, so Mother Bustle used to bake them just before he came, and she put them out on her kitchen window-sill to cool whilst she went upstairs to put on a pretty dress.

Somebody else liked Mother Bustle's curranty buns, too. That was little Grumple Goblin, who lived in the cottage next door. He always knew when Mother Bustle was baking buns because they smelt so good. Then he would look out of his window and watch to see if the old dame put them out to cool. How delicious they looked!

Mother Bustle made them sugary on top, and she put plenty of currants inside. Grumple had tasted them once or twice, and he wished he could taste them again.

Then he discovered that Mother Bustle always went upstairs to change her dress after she had put out the buns to cool on the window-sill; and as her bedroom was at the front of the cottage and the kitchen was at the back, what could be easier than to take one or two buns off the sill when Mother Bustle was upstairs!

It was very easy. Each Saturday Grumple managed to take one or two buns off the sill. At first Mother Bustle didn't notice that any were gone. But when Grumple took four one Saturday she frowned.

'Now surely I made more buns than this!' she said and counted them. 'Yes – there are four gone! Oh dear, oh dear, surely nobody is so mean as to steal a few of my curranty buns from me!'

Well, the next Saturday four more buns went and Mother Bustle couldn't imagine who could be stealing them. She was sure it wasn't Mr Hoo-Ha, who lived on her right. And it couldn't be the Grumple Goblin, surely, because he was always so polite and well-mannered. He always lifted his hat to her, shook hands politely, and asked how she was. No, no – it couldn't be the Grumple Goblin!

Well, then, who could it be? It must be some bad imp who had seen her buns on the sill and came each Saturday to take them. Mother Bustle wondered what to do about it.

Then she smiled a little to herself. 'I know,' she said, 'I'll make my buns as usual – but I'll put some magic glue on the top of them instead of that sugary stickiness! What a shock for the thief!'

So the next Saturday she baked a batch of buns and on some of them she spread some strong magic glue.

She put these to cool out on the window-sill. The others she put to cool in the larder. Then she went upstairs as usual to change her dress.

Grumple saw the buns on the sill. Not so many as usual! He wouldn't dare to take more than two. He crept along quietly, keeping behind the bushes. He put his hands up to take two of the buns. Ah – that felt a big one – and that one, too!

Off he went to his cottage with them, and put them down on a plate. But wait – he couldn't put them down! They stuck to his hands! He couldn't get them off.

'Gracious goodness, what's happened!' said Grumple in alarm. 'That silly old woman has put too much sugar on them! They're as sticky as glue!' It was no use. He couldn't get the buns off his hands. In the end he had to go out and ask Billy the goat to eat the buns away from his hands. Billy was quite pleased to do this. But even when the buns had gone the sticky stuff was still there.

Grumple couldn't pick up anything without it sticking to him. He was really in despair. He looked at his sticky hands and suddenly felt sure that there was some kind of magic in the stickiness. He must get rid of it at once. He couldn't go on, day after day, with hands as sticky as this!

He thought he would go and see his sister, the Artful Goblin. She would be sure to know a spell to take the stickiness away. She would probably want him to do something difficult for her in return, but Grumple couldn't help that; and, anyway, he could always break his promise – a little thing like that wouldn't bother Grumple. So off he went to his sister's.

And who should be coming along to go to tea with Mother Bustle but Policeman Plod-Along, thinking joyfully of strong tea and curranty buns! He saw the Grumple Goblin and smiled at him. Mother Bustle had often told him of the polite, well-mannered goblin. He held out his hand to Grumple.

'Good afternoon!' he said. 'I'm so pleased to see you. How do you do!'

Grumple shook hands without thinking – and then to his horror he found that he couldn't pull away his hand! The stickiness on it made it stick fast to Policeman Plod-Along's hand!

'Hey! What's this! Hey, leave go! Don't be silly, Grumple.'

'I'm not silly. I just can't help it,' said Grumple, pulling hard. 'Oh, it hurts! I'm stuck to you and you're stuck to me!'

'Well, you'll have to come along to Mother Bustle's to see if she can unstick us,' said Plod-Along, and he and Grumple walked hand in hand to Mother Bustle's. Grumple didn't want to go in at all, but he had to. Where Plod-Along went he had to go, too!

Mother Bustle was surprised to see the two coming hand in hand. 'Well, well – are you such close friends?' she cried. 'How do you do, Grumple?'

But Grumple couldn't let go Plod-Along's hand

to shake hands with Mother Bustle! Plod-Along explained to his sister.

'You see, there's some sticky magic on his hand,' he said. 'Can't make it out! Can you do anything about it?'

Mother Bustle's sharp eyes went to Grumple's red face. 'Oho! OHO!' she cried. 'I think I know where that sticky magic came from. Yes, I think I know. For shame, Grumple! Did you take my buns?'

'Buns? What buns?' said Grumple, pretending he knew nothing.

'Oh, well – if you didn't take them it can't be my sticky-magic,' said Mother Bustle. 'I shan't be able to take it away then.'

Grumple looked in desperation at Mother Bustle's grim face. He couldn't be fastened like this to Plod-Along all his life! No, he really couldn't!

'Well – I did take your buns,' he said. 'But I'll pay for them. So just you set me free, you horrid old woman! Then I can get my purse out!'

'WHAT'S THIS?' roared Plod-Along suddenly. 'You've been taking my sister's buns? Stealing them! So you're a thief, are you? Come along to the police-station with me at once!'

Well, Grumple had to go, of course, because he couldn't take his hand away from Plod-Along's! Mother Bustle went with them, and as soon as Grumple was safely in prison she poured some magic water over his hands and away went the stickiness at once! His hand fell away from the policeman's, and Plod-Along went outside the door and locked him in.

'Let him spend a night there,' said Mother Bustle. 'Just to teach him a lesson, the wicked little creature! So polite and well-mannered – and so bad-hearted underneath. I'm sure it is he who has been taking Dame Click's eggs and Mother Lucy's washing off her line!'

Grumple spent a lonely night locked up. In the morning he was allowed to go home, looking scared and miserable. When he got there Mother Bustle popped her head over the wall.

'Well, Grumple, let this be a lesson to you! And remember this – if ever I think you're taking things that don't belong to you again you'll find your hands as sticky as you did yesterday! So just you be careful!'

Mother Bustle still puts her curranty buns out on her window-sill to cool every Saturday – but since that time she hasn't missed a single bun. Grumple doesn't dare to go near them!

Pretty-Star
the Pony

Pretty-Star the Pony

I am a little black pony, and my name is Pretty-Star because I have a pretty white star right in the middle of my forehead.

I used to live in Farmer White's field, and eat the sweet grass there. I didn't like Farmer White, for he was a rough man with a loud voice that made me jump with fright. When he rode me I felt as if my back was going to give way, for he was so heavy. He gave me the whip, too, and that is enough to break any willing pony's heart, for I never needed it.

A little girl called Mary used to come and see me every day. She lived in a house near to Farmer White's and went to school on her bicycle every morning. On her way there and back she would stop and speak to me. Sometimes she brought me lumps of sugar, or an apple.

'I wish you were *my* pony,' she would say. 'I would love to have you for my very own. I would ride you to school every day, and look after you well, dear little Pretty-Star. When my birthday comes I am going to ask my Daddy to buy you for me.'

One day her bicycle had a puncture, so she came and asked Farmer White if he would lend me to her to ride to school on. He said yes, so she put my saddle and bridle on, and jumped up on my back. How proud I was to carry her! I neighed gladly, and trotted along carefully. She was as light as a feather, and didn't pull at my mouth a bit. She talked to me all the way, and though I couldn't answer her in her own language, I loved to hear her voice.

She gave me an apple and tied me up to the school gate in the shade of a tree, just within reach of some nice juicy grass. There I waited patiently until she came out to go home again.

'Oh, Pretty-Star, I *wish* you were my very own pony,' she said, when she let me loose in Farmer White's field again. 'I am sure we should love each other dearly.'

When her birthday came she brought her father to see me.

'Daddy, will you give me this little black pony for my birthday?' she asked. 'I want him more than anything else in the world.'

'But what would you do with him?' asked her father. 'You've got your bicycle to ride to school on. You'd soon get tired of having to look after a real live pony. It's not like a bicycle, you know, Mary. You couldn't just put him in a shed and leave him there till you wanted him. He would have to be fed, and groomed carefully.'

'Yes, Daddy,' said Mary. 'I know just how to groom him, and I could take care of him much better than

Farmer White does, really I could. He doesn't care a bit for him.'

I nuzzled my nose into Mary's hand, and looked at her father pleadingly, for I wanted to belong to Mary. But the big man shook his head.

'No,' he said. 'I must disappoint you, Mary. The pony is quite a nice little thing, but he is not worth the price Farmer White is asking. I'll buy you a big doll instead.'

Mary didn't say any more, but she gave me a hug and a kiss, and I knew better than her father how sad she was not to have me for her own.

Mary got her big doll, but she wouldn't play with it. She was the sort of person who likes real live pets that love her back when she loves them. She came to see me every day, and I whinnied a welcome, and ran to meet her.

One day she came to the nearby river to fish with her big boy cousin. I stood as near to them as I could, but I couldn't get very near because of a high hedge in between. Mary waved to me when she saw my head over the hedge, and I whinnied back.

I watched them all the morning. They didn't catch any fish, and the big boy was impatient.

'Let's climb up on this rock where there's a deep, quiet pool beneath,' he said. 'I'm sure there are plenty of fish there, Mary.'

'We must be careful then,' said Mary. 'It is dangerous to climb up there, my Daddy says.'

I knew it was, too, and I watched them anxiously. They had just reached the top of the rock when Mary slipped. She clutched at the boy and missed him. Then she fell right over the rock and I heard her fall *splash!* into the deep pool below.

'Mary, Mary!' called the boy. 'Can you swim?'

I knew she wasn't able to, but of course I couldn't tell him that. I was so anxious that I didn't know what to do. I couldn't get out of my field, for the gate was shut, and I ran whinnying round and round and round, thinking of Mary in the water. I hoped the boy would dive in and rescue her, but he didn't.

I suddenly saw him start running off towards the house where Mary lived. He was calling 'Help! Help! Mary is in the water!' as he ran.

Well, I knew that the little girl would drown if no one rescued her soon, and I was almost mad with grief. I decided to get to the river if I only could. So I ran backwards a few paces, then galloped full tilt at the high hedge. Over I went, with my hoofs just touching the top. I have never jumped so high before, and I don't suppose I ever shall again.

Once over the hedge I raced down to the river. I looked into the water, and soon saw where Mary was. She was holding on to a broken bough of a tree that dipped down to the river, and I knew that it would soon break off altogether, and then my little friend would drown.

I jumped straight into the river myself, and began to swim towards Mary. I had nearly got to her when the bough broke right off, and the little girl went under the water. She came up spluttering and gasping – but she saw me.

'Help me, Pretty-Star!' she cried – then down she went again.

In a trice I was up to her. I plucked hold of her wet clothes with my strong teeth, and pulled her up. She came up spluttering again, and caught hold of my neck.

'Hold on tightly,' I said in my horse language that she understood so well. So she held on whilst I turned myself carefully round in the water, and began to swim for the shallow bank. The current was against me, and it was very difficult. I am only a little pony, and Mary seemed very heavy, with all her wet clothes dragging her down. I began to gasp and pant myself, and I felt as if my heart was bursting in two.

Then I saw some people running towards the river. There was the boy and Mary's father and mother, and the gardener, too, carrying a rope. They all ran to the bank, and looked down on Mary and me.

'The pony's got her! He must have jumped right over the hedge!' cried Mary's father in amazement.

'Oh, the brave little pony!' cried Mary's mother, with tears streaming down her cheeks.

Just at that moment I reached the bank, and stumbled out of the water. I was so exhausted that I had to lie down in the mud. Mary's father picked her up and cuddled her, and her mother cried tears all over her.

'I'm all right, Daddy,' said Mary. 'But just look at that poor little tired pony. I'm sure he must nearly have burst his heart in two, swimming against the river like that.'

Fancy her knowing that! That just shows how she loved me. Of course, I soon felt better, then, dear me, the petting I had! It was wonderful!

Nobody could make enough of me. I had sugar and apples, and everyone stroked my nose and patted me. It was lovely.

But the nicest reward of all was still to come.

'Mary, we'll take the pony back to Farmer White now,' said her father. 'And if he's still willing to sell him, you shall have him. He deserves to belong to you, for I never saw such a plucky little creature in my life!'

Farmer White said he was quite willing to sell me. So Mary's father paid for me that same day, and Mary rode on my back to her home. I was her very own pony at last!

And now I am as happy as the day is long, for I take Mary to and from school every day, and we always go for a long ride together in the evenings. On Saturdays we go out all day long together, and on Sundays I take her to church. Don't you think I am a very lucky little pony?

The Stolen Shadow

The Stolen Shadow

Mark and Rachel were very happy. They were going for a picnic, and they had walked to Pixie Hill in the warm sunshine. Mark carried a bag in which was a bottle of lemonade, two apples and a book, and Rachel carried one with some sandwiches, two pieces of cake and a slab of chocolate.

'Isn't it fun to go off alone like this!' said Rachel. 'Just ourselves – no one to say "Don't!" No one to say "Now mind you're good".'

'We'll have a picnic on the side of Pixie Hill,' said Mark. 'I'm getting hungry – aren't you? Wasn't it nice of Mummy to pack us such a lovely lunch!'

They went up the hill. There were gorse bushes there and soft heather. Bracken grew around too, and a few pretty silver birches. Mark looked round for a nice place to sit.

'Look at that little clearing over there,' he said, pointing to a round piece of grass under a silver birch. 'Let's go there. If we sit in the heather we shan't be able to stand our lemonade bottle up properly.'

They went to the round patch of grass and sat down. Soon they had spread out their feast and were busy eating it.

'Rachel!' said Mark, suddenly. 'I thought I saw something moving in the heather over there. Maybe it was a bird or a rabbit – but it seemed to have a *face*!'

'Ooh! Was it a pixie, do you suppose?' said Rachel excitedly. 'They were once believed to live on this hill, you know! Look again, Mark!'

'There it is!' said Mark, and he pointed. Rachel saw a mischievous little face peeping out of the heather.

Then out hopped a small pixie, with a large pair of scissors!

'Good day to you,' he said in a high, twittering voice, like a bird's. 'Will you sell me something?'

'It depends what you want,' said Mark, staring at the pixie in surprise.

'I want a shadow,' said the pixie. 'My master, the Enchanter Bushy-Brow, needs one to make a spell. So he has sent me out to buy a nice black shadow. I will give you one golden piece if I may cut off yours!'

'You can't cut a shadow off!' said Mark. 'You know you can't!'

'You can't with ordinary scissors,' said the pixie. 'But you can with these. They have been dipped in magic and can cut anything! Watch me cut this tree's shadow!'

He ran to where the shadow of the silver birch tree waved on the ground. He snipped with his scissors – and hey presto, they cut the shadow, and the pixie tossed it over to the astonished children.

'There you are!' he said. 'What did I say?'

Rachel picked up the little shadow snippet. It was cold, light and soft and silky as spider thread. It was like nothing she had ever seen, and shone now purple, now black.

'Well!' she said. 'This is very strange. But, pixie, I'm sorry, you can't possibly cut either of our shadows. We should hate to be without them. They follow us wherever we go. We shouldn't feel real without them, you know. Sometimes they are long, and sometimes they are short – but they are always there, as long as there is any daylight or light of any kind!'

The pixie looked sulky. He made a rude face at the children, hopped back into the heather and disappeared.

'I don't think I like that pixie much,' said Rachel. 'But fancy seeing one, Mark! How awfully exciting!'

'I wonder if he has a little house in that heather,' said Mark. 'Let's go and look.'

The two children left the shade of the birch tree and

went towards the heather. Their shadows stretched dark behind them, for the sun was very strong.

They peered down into the heather. They did not hear a tiny burst of laughter, nor did they see the small pixie creeping behind them with his big scissors.

He ran to the edge of Rachel's short shadow. Snip-snip-snip went his scissors, and soon he had cut her shadow all round the edge!

Then he gave two sharp snips by her feet – and he had her shadow. Quick as lightning he rolled it up, tucked it under his arm, and fled off, laughing like a little waterfall.

Mark looked round at once, for he knew it was the pixie. 'Look, Rachel, look!' he cried. 'It's the pixie again! What's that he's got under his arm?'

'Oh, oh! It's my shadow!' said Rachel, looking down at her feet. 'See, Mark, there's *your* shadow – but there isn't one for me. That horrid, horrid little thing snipped mine away when we were looking into the heather just now!'

'Oh, Rachel, how dreadful!' said Mark, staring down at Rachel's feet. 'You do look strange without a shadow. Whatever shall we do?'

'We must get it back!' said Rachel, and she began to run after the pixie. 'Come on, Mark, quick! I'm going to lose my shadow. Hurry!'

They tore off, and the running pixie heard them. He ran to a small yellow door set closely into the hillside, opened it, and disappeared. The door slammed.

'Quick! He's gone in here!' said Mark, and he banged at the door. It opened, and a rabbit looked out. She had a large apron on, and big glasses that kept slipping down her nose.

'Oh!' she said in surprise.

'Oh!' said both children, just as surprised.

'What do you want?' asked the rabbit. 'First a pixie bursts into my house, slams the door and runs out the back way – and now you come banging. On my baking morning too!'

'So sorry!' said Mark, stepping inside. 'But tell us where that pixie went. He's got my sister's shadow.'

'Oh, the mischief,' said the rabbit, putting her glasses on her forehead. 'He's a rogue, he is. He came last week and wanted two of my whiskers for something, and the faces he made at me when I told him to grow some of his own, and cut those.'

She shook her head and her glasses slid down her nose again. She pointed to her back door.

'He went out there,' she said. 'Hurry up, and you'll catch him!'

The children shot out of the door, and to their enormous surprise found themselves in a large open field, instead of inside the hill. They looked all about – but not a sign of the pixie was to be seen!

'Bother!' said Rachel. 'Where's he gone?'

'To Bushy-Brow the Enchanter, I suppose!' said Mark gloomily. 'We shall never get him now, Rachel. He has got too big a start, and we don't know which way he went.'

'Well, we know where he's going, don't we!' said Rachel. 'If we find the way to the Enchanter's, we might get there first, and stop him just as he's going in!'

'Good idea!' said Mark. 'We'll ask the way, as soon as we see someone.'

'Look, we'll ask this person,' said Rachel. 'He looks like a gnome.' It *was* a gnome – he came shuffling over the field towards them, his long beard nearly reaching the ground. He muttered something as he went, and the children felt half afraid of speaking to him.

'Threepence and twopence and a penny, how much change from tenpence?' they heard him say. 'Threepence and twopence and a penny, how much—'

'The answer is fourpence,' said Mark.

'Ooh!' said the gnome, startled. He stopped and stared at Mark. 'Fourpence did you say? Ah, then I have the right change after all! I can cheer up! I thought I should have fivepence.'

'Can you tell us where Bushy-Brow the Enchanter

lives?' asked Mark, pleased to see the gnome smiling brightly.

'Certainly, certainly,' said the gnome. 'Do you see that hill over there? Go up it, take the mat at the top, slide to the bus, take the bus to the pond, hop on a duck and there you are!'

He went off, whistling cheerily.

'What funny directions,' said Rachel, puzzled. 'They sound quite mad to me.'

'Well, I suppose this must be part of Fairyland,' said Mark, 'so we must expect funny things. Come on. Let's go up that hill and see if there really is a mat at the top.'

'Slide to the bus, take the bus to the pond, hop on a duck and there you are!' repeated Rachel. 'Well, it's easy enough to remember!'

They ran to the hill and began to climb up. It was steep and they puffed and panted. When they got to the top they exclaimed in delight – for below them lay Fairyland, smiling in the sun! Castles and palaces, crooked houses and toadstool villages spread before them. It was a marvellous sight!

The two children gazed for a long time and were too delighted to say a word. Then they looked for the runaway pixie – but he was nowhere to be seen.

'Oh, Rachel, here's the mat! Do come and look!' cried Mark. Rachel ran to him – and sure enough, there was a large blue mat, hanging on a peg – and stretching down the hill in front was a long, steep, slippery slide!

'We go down the slide on the mat!' said Mark. 'Rachel, what fun!'

Before they could use the mat, a brownie came running up, unhitched the mat from the peg, set it at the top of the slide, and down he went, his hair streaming out behind him.

'Oh, now he has taken the mat!' said Rachel in disappointment. The brownie reached the bottom, threw the mat into the air, and, to the children's great astonishment, it flew up the hill again on a pair of butterfly-like wings! It hung itself on the peg, and closed its wings tightly, so that they could hardly be seen.

'Quick, before anyone else takes it,' said Mark. He caught up the mat and put it at the top of the slide. He and Rachel got on, and pushed off. Whoooooooosh! Down flew the mat at top speed, right to the very bottom. It was a most exciting feeling.

'I wish we could do that again,' said Mark, getting off. He threw the mat into the air, as he had seen the brownie do, and at once it spread its wings and flew up to the hilltop, where it once more hung itself up.

'Fairyland is much more exciting than *our* world!' said Rachel. 'Come on. We must look for the bus.'

'There it is, in front of you!' said Mark. 'You don't need to look for it!'

'Oh, isn't it small!' cried Rachel, in delight. So it was – very small indeed. It was painted yellow, and had bright red wheels, so it was very colourful. There was no conductor and no driver, so the children wondered what to do.

A large fat rabbit walked by, wheeling a pram with six baby rabbits in. Mark ran up to her.

'Please, what time does the bus go?' he asked.

'Any time you like,' said the rabbit, looking puzzled. 'Just get in if you want to and drive off!'

'Oh! Do you mean *we* can drive it?' asked Rachel, in delight. 'Well, where's the pond? We have to drive to that.'

'Just say "Pond" to the bus, and it'll know the way,' said the rabbit. Two of her baby rabbits began to cry, so she hurriedly said goodbye and wheeled her pram away, saying: 'Sh! Sh! Sh!'

'Isn't everything simply lovely here?' said Rachel. 'I should be perfectly happy if only I had my shadow back again!'

They climbed in at the front of the bus. Mark took hold of the wooden steering-wheel, and said 'Pond!' in his loudest voice. The bus shook itself, and began to trundle away down a narrow lane. It rumbled on for a long way, and at last ran down to a big pond. To the children's surprise it ran right into the water and floated towards some big ducks who were quacking together nearby.

When the ducks saw the children, two of them swam up at once. Mark and Rachel stepped neatly on to their backs, and the bus floated back to the bank. It got out, shook itself, and trundled back up the lane, gleaming in the sun. It was really a very good and clever little bus. The children felt quite sorry to see it go.

'Take us to Bushy-Brow the Enchanter,' said Mark to the duck.

'Quark!' said the duck, in a deep voice. 'Quark, quark!'

Instead of swimming, the ducks suddenly spread out big white wings and rose into the air. The children were so astonished, that they nearly fell off! Mark half slid off, and then, catching tight hold of the duck's neck, he pulled himself up again.

'Quark!' said the duck severely. 'If you do that sort of thing I shall choke! I could hardly breathe then.'

'So sorry,' said Mark humbly. He and Rachel sat very still after that, and looked down on the palaces and castles of Fairyland as they flew over them. At last the duck flew down to a strange tower-like house, set on the top of a hill.

'Quark!' said one of the ducks. 'Here you are!'

The children slipped off their feathery backs and looked at the tower-like building. The ducks flew away and left them there.

'How do we get in?' said Mark puzzled. 'There isn't any door!'

There certainly didn't seem to be! The children walked round and round – but no, not even the tiniest door was to be seen! Then they suddenly saw one!

It appeared before their very eyes – a bright blue one with a brass knocker! It opened – and out shot, who do you think? Yes – that mischievous pixie who had taken Rachel's shadow.

Someone kicked him out – and at the same time an angry voice cried: 'You meddlesome creature, you! You've spoilt my spell!'

Then the door shut – and immediately vanished again! The pixie sat up and began to cry. But as soon as he saw Mark and Rachel, he looked most astonished and stopped.

'How did you get here?' he asked.

'Never mind that!' said Mark in a cross voice. 'Tell me this – where's my sister's shadow that you stole, you wicked little creature?'

'Bushy-Brow has got it!' said the pixie with a grin. Mark looked so angry that his grin stopped and he jumped to his feet. Mark shot out his hand to get hold of him – but he dodged away, shouting: 'Can't catch *me*, can't catch *me*!'

'Let him be,' said Rachel in disgust. 'He is a most tiresome little fellow – but he hasn't got my shadow now, that's plain. Let's bang on the place where the door was, and see if we can get the Enchanter to speak to us.'

So they went to where the door had been and banged hard. A cross voice came from inside.

'If that's you again, pixie, I'll turn you into birdseed and give you to my canary!'

'It isn't the pixie,' said Mark. 'It's two children come to see you.'

At once the blue door appeared again, and was thrown open. The children saw a tall, kindly-faced old man, wearing an enormous pointed hat, and a curious black cloak that flowed round him like water.

'This is an honour and a pleasure!' he said. 'I don't often have children to visit me! Come in!'

The children went inside the towerhouse. It was small inside, but the ceiling was so high that they couldn't reach it. A fire burned in one corner and in the middle of the floor was a deep hole out of which came a bubbling noise and some strange yellow mist.

'Don't be frightened,' said Bushy-Brow. 'That's only where I make my spells,'

'Oh,' said Mark, 'isn't it strange.'

'It may be strange to *you*,' said Bushy-Brow politely, 'but quite ordinary to *me*.'

He smiled at Mark, and then stared hard at Rachel. He stared so hard that the little girl felt most uncomfortable. He looked at her feet, he looked at her face, then he looked back at her feet again.

'Little girl,' he said in a puzzled voice, 'there is something very strange about you – you have no shadow! Did you know this?'

'Oh, yes,' said Rachel. 'Of course I know. That wicked little pixie of yours stole it from me this morning. He snipped it off with his scissors!'

'Stars and moon! So it was *your* shadow he brought,' cried Bushy-Brow. 'He told me it was the shadow of an old woman who didn't want hers any more. The naughty little creature! I'll certainly turn him into birdseed.'

'Oh, no, don't do that!' said Rachel. 'I really shouldn't like you to do that, although I don't like the pixie a bit. But I *would* like my shadow back, please!'

'My dear little girl, I've used it in that spell you see being made at this very minute!' said the Enchanter, and he pointed to where the strange yellow mist came up from the bubbling hole in the floor.

'Oh, I say! *Now* what shall I do?' said poor Rachel, with tears in her eyes. 'I *must* have a shadow!'

'You shall have one!' said Bushy-Brow, patting her on the back, kindly. 'Don't cry! I wouldn't have used your shadow for worlds, if I'd known it was yours.'

He went to the door and stared out. 'Pippetty, Pippetty!' he called. 'Come here! I want you!'

The naughty little pixie came running up. The Enchanter took hold of him and marched him into the tall room.

'This little girl says you took her shadow,' he said sternly. 'I have used it in my spell, thinking it was an old woman's. You are a wicked fellow, Pippetty. I shall take away *your* shadow and give it to this little girl!'

The pixie began to cry, but it was no use. The Enchanter took some big scissors and neatly snipped away all the pixie's purple-black shadow. Then he smacked him and sent him outside, looking very strange without his shadow!

The Enchanter took a needle and threaded it with purple silk. Then he picked up the shadow and went to Rachel.

'Oh dear, are you going to sew it on me?' said the little girl, frightened. 'Will it hurt?'

'Not a bit!' said Bushy-Brow. He dug the needle into his hand, and then into Rachel – she couldn't feel the slightest prick!

'It's magic!' he said.

He bent down and swiftly sewed the little shadow to Rachel's feet, watered it with something from a can, and then muttered some strange words. The shadow stretched itself, shivered a bit, and then lay still.

'It's yours now,' said the Enchanter. 'A bit small for you, perhaps – but no one will notice. Once a year, on Midsummer's Night, it will try to get away from you to go to the pixies' ball, but just wish a wish, and it will be still again.'

'Wish a wish!' said Rachel in delight. 'Will it come true?'

'Of course,' said the Enchanter. 'Try a wish now, if you like, and see.'

'I wish we were home!' said Rachel, at once – and hey presto, there came an enormous wind that caught them up, twisted them round seven times and set them down again – in their very own garden! What do you think of that?

'I can't believe it!' cried Rachel.

'Oh, Rachel, why did you wish us away?' said Mark. 'We were having such a great time!'

'Never mind! I've got one wish every year!' said Rachel. 'I'll wish us back again, if you like, next Midsummer's Night! Oh, what fun! I'm glad, glad, glad I've got a pixie-shadow instead of my own!'

'You must be the only girl in the world who has!'

said Mark. 'I wish I had too!'

'Perhaps I'll wish one for you too, one year,' said Rachel. 'Come on – let's go and tell Mummy all about it!'

They did – and Mummy said yes, it was perfectly true, Rachel's shadow *was* small for her – and the shadow's ears always looked pointed, like a pixie's. Isn't it strange?

On Jimmy's Birthday

On Jimmy's Birthday

Jimmy was looking forward to his birthday. Mummy always gave the children a lovely time then. She had promised Jimmy a party, with a big cake and candles. She had bought boxes of crackers and put them away.

Jimmy told Jill about them, and about the cake Mummy was going to make. Jill was his sister, and she was looking forward to Jimmy's birthday.

'Baby is too little to know about birthdays yet,' said Jimmy. 'He's only had one birthday and that was the day he was born. I hope he won't mind the crackers popping off.'

Then something sad happened. The day before

Jimmy's birthday Baby fell ill. Mummy was very worried and she called in the doctor.

'You must keep the baby very, very quiet,' said the doctor, looking grave. 'Don't let the others bother him or make a noise. He must sleep all he can.'

After the doctor had gone Mummy spoke to Jimmy and Jill. 'I'm sorry, dears,' she said, 'but I'm afraid that as Baby is so ill we must put off the party tomorrow. It would be too noisy – and the crackers would frighten him, poor mite.'

Jimmy was dreadfully disappointed. Birthdays and birthday parties only came once a year, and on birthdays you couldn't help feeling happy and noisy. Now he and Jill would have to creep about, and not laugh loudly, nor even have anyone in the house.

'Be brave about it, Jimmy,' said Mummy, seeing how sad both children looked. 'I'm so worried about Baby. You must help me, if you can, and we'll have the party when Baby is better.'

Jimmy put his arms around his mother. 'Don't you

worry about my birthday!' he said, and he tried to smile. 'That doesn't matter a bit!'

But it did matter, of course, and when his birthday morning came, and Mummy was too worried about Baby to make a fuss of him, Jimmy felt very sad. He had to go round to all his friends and tell them not to come to the party. On the way back Jill and Jimmy met old Mr Benny. He was carrying a basket full of shopping which looked much too heavy for him.

Jimmy ran up to him and took the basket. 'I'll carry it,' he said. 'We are going your way.'

'Thank you, thank you!' said old Mr Benny, twinkling his blue eyes at them. 'You're always such a well-mannered boy, Jimmy. Now – let me see – surely it is your birthday today! Are you having a party?'

Then Jimmy told him about Baby being so ill, and Mr Benny listened and nodded. 'So I'm not really keeping my birthday today,' said Jimmy.

'But I can't have a birthday wasted like that!' said Mr Benny. '*I'll* have a party for you!'

'Oh, Mr Benny – but your house is much too small for a party!' said Jimmy. And indeed Mr Benny's cottage was only just big enough to take him and his old black cat!

'I won't have it at my house!' said Mr Benny. 'I'll have it at the Zoo! I'll hire a big car and we'll take you and your friends in it to the Zoo! Yes, and we'll take your birthday cake and crackers, too, and have them on the lawn there. We can buy lemonade and sandwiches and buns!'

'Oh – do you really mean it?' said Jill and Jimmy together.

'Of course. Go round to your friends again and tell them to come to my house at half-past two,' said Mr Benny. 'And you bring your cake and crackers!'

So off they all went to the Zoo that afternoon, chattering and laughing in the big car that Mr Benny had ordered.

'Going to the Zoo is an even bigger birthday treat than a party!' said Jimmy, happily. And it was! They saw all the animals, and they gave the monkeys bananas and oranges, and Mr Benny gave the keeper a tin of treacle for the brown bears. What fun it was to see them licking out the treacle, grunting with joy all the time.

'They're enjoying Jimmy's birthday too!' said Jill and everyone laughed.

Then they had a lovely picnic and ate the birthday cake up, every scrap. It was most delicious. They drank lemonade and orangeade, and then Mr Benny said it was quite time that they all had a ride on the elephants.

Nobody wanted to go home. 'Well, of course, you can stay here if you like, and be shut up with the monkeys at closing-time,' said Mr Benny, smiling. 'But I think you'd better come home with me, really.'

Jimmy and Jill thanked the kind old man for the birthday treat. 'It's a pleasure to do anything for well-mannered children!' said old Mr Benny. 'I've enjoyed it all too!'

When they got home Mummy met them with a smiling face. 'Baby's much better!' He slept all day long. I'm so glad you had such a happy birthday, Jimmy. You did deserve it, and now you've still got your party to look forward to, haven't you?'

He's having it tomorrow – and he's asking Mr Benny, of course. Have a good time, Jimmy!

Bonzo Gets
into Trouble

Bonzo Gets into Trouble

Bonzo was a rough-haired fox-terrier. He was a clever little fellow, and very fond of his little master, Peter, and of his big master, Peter's father.

He would do anything in the world for them. He played ball when they wanted a game. He lay quietly by the fire when they wanted to read. He walked for miles with them when they wanted a walk. He welcomed them with delight whenever they came home from school or from business, and jumped up and barked at the top of his voice to show them how glad he was to see them.

One Saturday afternoon Peter's father said they

would bath Bonzo in the sunny garden.

'He is dreadfully dirty,' he said to Peter. 'He really must have a bath. Get the old tin bath out of the shed, Peter, and I'll get some pails of hot water.'

'I'd better catch Bonzo first,' said Peter. 'He hates baths, and he'll run away and hide if he sees the bath coming!'

But Bonzo had already heard the dreadful word 'bath'! He ran into the kitchen and hid under the table. Peter found him there and tied him up to the table-leg to stop him hiding anywhere else.

'You stay there and be a good dog,' he said. 'We'll make you so nice and clean that Mummy won't even mind you sitting in the best armchair!'

Peter went to get the tin bath. Then he found the shampoo, the scrubbing brush and the old towel. His father was carrying pails of hot water to and fro.

Bonzo watched angrily. Why couldn't he be dirty? It was nice to be dirty. A bath was a horrible thing to have. He wouldn't have one – no, he wouldn't!

He'd bite through his lead and get away!

He began to gnaw his leather lead. He bit and nibbled, gnawed and tugged – and at last, hurrah, it was in half! He gave a yelp and tore out of the door. He knew a fine hiding-place in the garden bushes. He would go there and wait until Peter and his father were tired of calling him.

Off he went, and managed to get to the bushes without anyone seeing him. He sat down and kept as quiet as a mouse.

Soon the bath was ready. 'Get Bonzo!' called Father. Peter went to get him – but dear me, he was gone! There was the lead bitten in half, and no Bonzo!

'Oh, Daddy, isn't he naughty? He's gone!' cried Peter. 'He's bitten his nice new lead in half, and now I shall have to open my money-box to buy a new one. Where do you suppose he is?'

'Goodness knows!' Father said crossly. 'I'll whistle him and perhaps he'll come.' So he whistled. But no Bonzo came. He heard the whistle quite clearly, but he thought of the bath waiting for him and he made up his doggy mind that he wasn't going to move!

Peter whistled. His father whistled again. Then he called, 'Bonzo! Bonzo! Come here, Bonzo!'

Then Peter called, 'Bonzo, Bonzo, Bonzo! Good dog! Where are you? Bonzo, come here!'

No Bonzo came. Father called again, getting really very cross, 'Bonzo! Bonzo! Bonzo! *Bonzo!*'

Bonzo trembled to hear such a big voice, but he didn't move. He crouched down in the bushes and waited.

Peter's father was very angry. He began to look for Bonzo. He hunted everywhere and so did Peter. The bath water got colder and colder. Soon it was too cold to be of any use.

At last Peter and his father gave up looking for the naughty little dog. They emptied the water out of the bath and went indoors. Bonzo crept out of the bushes and went to the open window. He lay down underneath to listen to what they were saying in the room beyond. Were they very angry with him?

'That wretched little dog is a perfect nuisance,' said Father. 'It's too late for you to go and fetch me my magazine now, Peter. I must go without it.'

'Oh, Daddy, let me go,' said Peter. 'It won't take me long.'

'No, you can't go now, Peter,' said his mother, looking up from her knitting. 'I'll be getting our tea ready in ten minutes.'

'I do think it's horrid of Bonzo to behave like this,' said Peter. 'I've got to buy him a new lead, and he's made Daddy and me waste all the nice sunny afternoon, and now poor Daddy can't have me fetch his magazine for him as I always do. I think Bonzo is a horrid, naughty little dog.'

Poor Bonzo! He felt as if his heart was breaking when he heard his little master speaking like that! He hadn't thought of Peter having to buy him a new lead – and he had quite forgotten about Peter always fetching his father's weekly magazine. Dear, dear, no wonder they thought him a horrid little dog. Well, he would go in and beg for forgiveness. Even if they told him off he wouldn't mind. He was so sorry about it.

So in at the door he crawled, his tail between his legs. Peter saw him and cried out in surprise, 'Look, Daddy, look, Mummy, here's Bonzo! I wonder where he was hiding. He looks awfully sorry for being so naughty.'

'Take no notice of him,' said Father. 'I shan't tell him off. It will be a much bigger punishment for him if we take no notice. Don't pat him or speak to him.'

So nobody spoke to Bonzo at all. Nobody patted him, nobody even looked at him. It was perfectly dreadful. Bonzo had such a pain round his heart that he really thought it must be breaking into small pieces. Whatever could he do to make his master and mistress love him again? Oh, how he wished he had never run away from his bath!

He licked the big master's fingers, but Father took

his hand away. He crawled over to Peter, but Peter wouldn't even look at him. He went to Mother, but she took no notice at all.

What could he do to make things right? How could he show everyone that he was sorry? He lay in a corner with his shaggy head on his paws and thought and thought.

And then he had a fine idea! He would go to the shop himself and get the magazine! He knew the way, and he could bring the magazine back in his mouth if he was careful not to bark.

Bonzo jumped up and went into the hall. He knew that Father always put a round yellowish thing called a pound on the hall table, which Peter took to the shop with him and gave the man in exchange for the magazine. He had better take that little round thing with him in case the man in the shop wanted it.

He jumped up on to a chair and tried to reach the pound coin with his mouth. He knocked it on to the floor and jumped down to pick it up. At last he managed to get it into his mouth. Off he went, out of the open kitchen door, the pound safely in his mouth.

It was quite a long way to the shop, but he got there at last. There was nobody in the shop except the owner, who was reading a book. Bonzo pushed open the door with his nose and went in. The man looked up.

'Hello, Bonzo,' he said. 'Is Peter coming for his father's magazine? I've got it here, ready for him.'

Bonzo jumped up and dropped the wet coin from his mouth on to the counter. The man was surprised. 'So you've carried the money for Peter, have you?' he said. 'Well, I never!'

The man waited for Peter to come, and when the little boy didn't arrive he went to the door and looked for him. He wasn't anywhere to be seen.

'That's funny,' said the man, puzzled. 'Where is Peter?'

Bonzo sat up and begged for the magazine. He thought the man was very stupid not to understand that he had come for the magazine. The man picked up the pound coin from the counter and scratched his head, puzzled. What ought he to do?

'Wuff!' barked Bonzo impatiently. 'Wuff, wuff!' The man suddenly took up the magazine he had put ready for Peter, folded it and held it out to Bonzo. In a trice the little dog snatched it from him, held it firmly in his mouth and trotted out of the shop. The man gaped in astonishment and ran to the door to watch him scamper down the street.

Bonzo raced home. He didn't talk to a single dog on the way because he was so afraid that if he opened his mouth to bark he would drop the paper. He still had it safely in his mouth when he reached home. He ran in at the kitchen door and went into the living-room. He went up to Peter's father, his tail wagging hard, and dropped the magazine into his lap.

Father picked it up in astonishment and looked at it. 'Look!' he said. 'Bonzo's brought me my magazine! Do you think he's been to the shop for it?'

'Wuff, wuff, wuff!' said Bonzo, frisking round, longing to be patted.

'I'll see if the money is gone from the hall,' said Peter's mother. She went, and came back saying, yes, it had gone! Then the telephone rang, and it was the man ringing up from his shop to tell Peter's father about how Bonzo had come to his shop with a pound and had taken the magazine!

'I'll call Peter,' said Father. 'We must tell him about Bonzo going to the newsagent's on his own.'

So Peter came downstairs, and dear me, how surprised he was to hear what Bonzo had done.

'I know why he did it, Daddy,' he said. 'He heard us talking about the magazine, and he made up his mind to go and fetch it to show us he was sorry for being so naughty about his bath. Didn't you, Bonzo?'

'Wuff, wuff, wuff!' barked Bonzo, and licked Peter's hand in joy.

'Well, well, we must forgive him,' said Father, stroking the happy little dog. 'He was certainly very clever to think of doing that! And fancy his taking the money, too! I think he had better go and fetch my magazine every week, Peter, as he knows so well how to do it! It will save you going.'

Bonzo was very happy. Peter's father patted him, his mother stroked him, and Peter tickled his neck. Everybody loved him again, and he wasn't in disgrace any more.

And now every Saturday he goes to fetch Father's magazine for him. He takes the pound coin in his mouth and brings back the magazine neatly folded. The man in the shop thinks he is a very clever dog, and each week at the shop if you were there you would find three or four people waiting for Bonzo to come, so that they might see him do his little bit of shopping!

Tomorrow Bonzo is going to have a bath. I do hope he won't run away again, and get himself in disgrace!

The Roundabout
Man

The Roundabout Man

The fair had come to the town. It was in the big field at one end of the town, and the children eagerly watched all the tents being put up, and the swings and hoopla, and oh, the big roundabout!

It was a most magnificent roundabout. There were animals to ride on, and these animals went up and down as well as round and round.

'It's just the nicest kind of roundabout there is,' said all the children.

'If I went on, I'd ride the camel,' said Judy to her twin, Jane. 'What would you ride, Jane?'

'That lovely swan,' said Jane. 'Then I should

pretend I was sailing and flying at the same time, going up and down, up and down, and round and round.'

'It's a pity Mummy's ill in hospital,' said Judy. 'She'd give us some money and let us go to the fair. But Auntie Nina won't, I'm sure. She never gives us anything, even when we run lots of errands for her.'

Auntie Nina did not believe in giving a lot of money to children. She believed in them paying for things themselves, and saving up if they wanted anything.

'You have your pocket money,' she said, 'and that should be enough. If you want anything, you must save up for it.'

So when Judy and Jane asked if they might go to the fair, and please could they have the money, Auntie Nina said, 'What about your pocket money? That is given to you to spend on things like the fair.'

'Well, Auntie,' said Judy, 'we haven't got any money at all till this Saturday, and then we want to spend it on something else.'

Judy and Jane had spent their pocket money on

buying flowers to take to their mother in hospital, and they each wanted to take her a bunch of primroses that week. But that meant there wouldn't be even a penny left.

Auntie Nina shook her head. 'I can't give you any more money,' she said. 'I'm sorry. I don't believe in handing out money to children whenever they ask for it. You have plenty of pocket money. If you can't save it up, you must go without things you want!'

There was no more to be said. Judy and Jane turned away sadly. Now they wouldn't go to the fair, and they would never ride on that lovely roundabout.

'I wouldn't mind not doing anything else at the fair, if only we could ride on the roundabout,' Judy said that evening, as they peeped over the hedge and watched the lions, tigers, swans, camels and bears going round and round and round to the sound of merry music. 'I just love that roundabout!'

They were on an errand for Auntie Nina. They had to go all the way to the farm for some eggs. It was a long way, and they had to be home for supper, so they couldn't stop long to watch the fair. They soon ran off, and made their way over the fields to the farm.

When they got there, the farmer's wife gave them the eggs and some hot biscuits from her oven. While they were eating them, a little old lady came into the farmhouse kitchen.

'Are you children going back to the town now?' she asked.

'Yes, we are,' said Judy.

'Well, then, I wonder if you'd take this parcel to my son for me,' said the old lady. 'It's his washing. He wants clean things for tomorrow, and I haven't been able to get out today because my legs have been bad. Could you take it for me, do you think? His lodgings are at the end of the High Street.'

Oh dear! That was a long way to go. They might be late for supper, too, and Auntie Nina would be angry. Still, they must help the old lady, and if they ran all the way they could do it.

So the twins took the parcel of washing and went. They ran all the way, panting, taking it in turns to carry the parcel, which was quite heavy.

When they got to the house in the High Street there was nobody in! They rang the bell and knocked loudly but no one came. The woman next door put her head out of the window and called to them. 'Who do you want?'

The twins looked at the name written on the parcel. 'We've got a parcel for Mr Tom Taylor,' said Jane.

'Oh, him! Well, you'll find him at the fair,' said the woman. 'I think he's with the swings.'

'Shall we take the parcel to him?' wondered Judy. 'Yes, we'd better. We can't leave it here on the doorstep!'

So they rushed off to the fairground. At the gate they said they had a parcel for Mr Tom Taylor, of the swings.

'Tom? Oh, he's the roundabout man,' said the woman at the gate. 'Over there, look. That man with the curly black hair.'

The twins went up to the curly-haired man. 'Well, do you want a ride?' he said.

'No,' said Judy. 'We've just brought you your washing. We went to the farm where your mother is staying, to get some eggs, and she asked us to bring you this parcel. But when we went to your lodgings there was nobody in, so we brought it to you here.'

'Well, what kind children!' said Mr Taylor. 'Who would have thought there were children who'd do a nice thing like that for a roundabout man! Wait a minute. I'll give you a pound for your kindness.'

'Oh, no thank you,' said Judy at once. 'We did it to help your mother. Our mother doesn't like us to take money for things like that.'

'Well, well, so you've got a mother as nice as yourself, have you?' said the roundabout man, putting the pound back in his pocket. 'But look here – you musn't be the only people doing a kindness.

I like being kind too, you know. Have you been on my roundabout?'

'No, never,' said the twins.

'Well, have a ride now,' said the roundabout man. 'Go on! Choose what animal you like!'

'We'd love to,' said Jane, looking longingly at the roundabout, which had just stopped. 'But we are awfully late. Our auntie, who's looking after us, will be cross if we aren't back for supper. We'll have to go.'

'You come back tomorrow,' said the roundabout man. 'Now, I won't take no for an answer! Will you promise me to come back tomorrow, and choose an animal to ride on?'

'Oh, we'd love to!' said the twins, joyfully. 'Thank you so much!'

They ran home, and were only just in time for supper. When they told their aunt all that had happened she was pleased.

'Well, if you want to go and get your little reward, you can go,' she said. 'You were very good children to refuse the pound he offered, and to come home without a ride so that you wouldn't be late. You deserve a treat. And why didn't you tell me you were spending all your pocket money on flowers for your mother? If I'd known that I would have given you some for the fair!'

Well, the next day Auntie Nina gave them a whole pound each, and off they went, full of delight.

They paid to go in, and when they got to the roundabout the curly-haired man greeted them joyously.

'Here you are then! I've been waiting for you. I'm going to let the roundabout have a very, very long go, just for you. Choose your animal, please.'

'We can pay for our ride after all,' said Judy. 'We've each got some money.'

'Now, look here!' said the roundabout man. 'Fair's fair! Did you let me pay you for your bit of kindness yesterday? No, you didn't. Then I shan't allow you to pay me for mine. Choose your animal.'

So Judy chose the camel she wanted and Jane chose the swan. The music began, the roundabout started to move. Up and down, up and down, went the camel and the swan, and round and round and round.

It was the very longest roundabout ride that anyone had ever known. I wish I'd been on it, too, don't you? I'd have chosen the lion, I think. What would you have had?

The Fairies' Shoemaker

The Fairies' Shoemaker

One very hot day Marjorie was going down the path by the cornfield, wheeling her doll's pram. Josephine, her doll, sat in the pram, a dear little sunshade over her head. Marjorie thought she looked very nice indeed.

Suddenly the little girl stopped and looked down at her foot.

'Something is hurting me,' she said. 'I wonder what it is. Perhaps I've got a stone in my shoe.'

She sat down by the hedge and took off her left shoe. She held it upside down and shook it – but no stone fell out. Marjorie put her hand inside and felt all round.

'Oh, it's a horrid, nasty nail!' she said. 'No wonder it hurt me. Whatever shall I do? It's quite a mile to my home, and I shall never be able to walk all that way with a nail sticking into my foot. It's made a big hole in my stocking already.'

Still, there didn't seem anything else to do, so Marjorie put her shoe on again and began to walk along the path with her pram. But after a bit she stopped.

'I simply can't!' she said, with tears in her eyes. 'The nail is making a hole in my foot, now! What shall I do? I can't walk without a shoe, and if I'm late Mummy will be cross.'

She sat down and took off her shoe again. She picked up a stone and tried to hammer the nail down, but it wasn't a bit of good. It only seemed to make it worse.

Suddenly she heard a small voice just by her elbow.

'What's the matter?' said the voice.

Marjorie looked round in surprise, and saw the funniest little man. He had a long beard, and wore a pointed cap and pointed shoes. Covering his tunic was a leather apron, and in his hand he held a shining tool.

'I've got a nail in my shoe,' said Marjorie, 'and I don't know how to walk home.'

'Well, fancy that!' said the little man, with a smile. 'You couldn't have chosen a luckier place to sit down in. You're just by my cobbler's shop!'

Marjorie looked where he was pointing and saw a little bench by the hedge, with scores of pairs of shoes lying about. Pieces of gay coloured leather lay on the ground.

'I make and mend shoes,' said the cobbler. 'For the fairies, of course, not for girls and boys. Shall I take the nail out of your shoe for you, or hammer it down?'

'But how can you?' asked Majorie. 'My shoe is as big as your whole shop! You haven't a hammer that would be big enough to knock my nail in.'

'Oh, that's easy,' said the cobbler, and he sang a few

strange words, tapping Marjorie's shoe all the time. To her great astonishment it became smaller and smaller and was at last so tiny that the cobbler took it into his hand. He ran to his bench, sat down upon it with his legs crossed and set to work to hammer down the nail. Marjorie watched him, very excited at such an adventure. Presently the little cobbler handed her back the shoe.

'It's done!' he said. 'It certainly was a nasty nail, but I've knocked it right down now, and it can't hurt you any more. You'll be able to walk home quite all right.'

'Oh, thank you,' said Marjorie. 'Are you going to make my shoe big for me again?'

'Yes,' said the cobbler, and once more he sang strange words, tapping Marjorie's shoe all the time. It grew bigger and bigger, and at last was the same size as before. Marjorie slipped it on and buttoned it. Then she stood up.

'Oh, that's quite all right now!' she said, joyfully.

'It is kind of you, little cobbler. Do tell me something I can do for you in return.'

'Well, you might tell me what that thing is called that your doll has got,' said the cobbler, pointing to the little sunshade over Josephine's head.

'That's a sunshade,' said Marjorie. 'It keeps the hot sun away, you know.'

'Well, I certainly must buy one,' said the cobbler. 'I get so dreadfully hot, sitting out here in the sun all day long. I'm sure I shall get sunstroke one day!'

'Let me give you this one,' said Marjorie, eagerly. 'It's just the right size for you.'

'Oh no, certainly not,' said the cobbler. 'No, no, I wasn't asking you for that one, little girl. I only wanted to know what it was called, so that I might buy one for myself.'

'You shall have this one!' said Marjorie, and she took it from her doll. 'Why, I've got two more at home, every bit as nice as this, little cobbler. Do have it, just to please me. You can't think how delighted I shall feel to think of you sitting under my little toy sunshade all day long, making shoes for the fairies!'

She stuck it firmly in the ground over the cobbler's bench. He was full of delight, and sat himself down underneath it with a joyful smile.

'It's fine!' he said, taking up a little shoe and beginning to sew a buckle on it. 'Why, it's as cool as cool can be under this sunshade. Thank you very much indeed, little girl. It's very kind of you. And by the way – if ever you want any shoes for your dolls, remember me, won't you? I only charge a penny a pair, and you can have them any colour you like.'

'I won't forget,' said Marjorie. 'Well, thank you very much for your kindness. I must say good-bye now, or I shall never get home!'

Off she went, wheeling her pram, leaving the little cobbler sitting under her doll's sunshade, whistling merrily at his work. 'I shall buy all my doll's shoes from him,' said Marjorie to herself. 'I'll give them a pair each on their birthdays.'

She did, – and everyone wants to know where she buys such beautiful little shoes. But Marjorie never tells them. It is such a lovely secret to keep to herself; so don't tell her I told you, will you?

Something Funny Going On

Something Funny
Going On

'Mrs Jones – we're going away for a week,' said Peter and Julie's mother to the plump little woman who came to help her each day. 'We shall lock up the house; but I wonder if you'd mind feeding Whiskers for us?'

'Feed your dear old cat – of course I will!' said Mrs Jones. 'It'll be a pleasure. I'll fetch fish from the shop and cook it myself for old Whiskers, and if you'll tell the milkman to leave some milk for him, I'll give him that, too. It won't take me more than a few minutes to pop across here and see to him.'

'Oh, thank you – you're kind!' said Peter. 'Whiskers

will be quite all right then. He's got his box in the little summerhouse, with his blanket.'

'He will be pleased to see you each day,' said Julie. 'Oh, I'm so glad you'll feed him. I'd quite made up my mind not to go away, if we couldn't get someone to look after him. Mummy, you'd have let me stay at home with him, wouldn't you?'

'No!' said Mother. 'You couldn't leave old Whiskers without someone to look after him – and I couldn't leave you here all alone! Anyway, he'll be all right now. He loves Mrs Jones.'

So the family said goodbye to Whiskers and went away quite happily. He didn't like them going, but he knew they would come back. They always did. He went to see if his comfortable little box was in the summerhouse. Yes, it was – and his blanket, too. Now he would be quite all right!

Mrs Jones kept her word. She brought a plate of fish each day, and poured out some milk for Whiskers as well. She had a quick look round the outside of the house to make sure that everything was all right.

On the third day she fed Whiskers as usual, and then hurried down the garden path to go home. She had to pass a little shed on the way, where the children's father kept his pots and tools and brooms and other gardening things. She was almost past the shed, when she suddenly stopped.

Had she heard something as she passed the shed? Surely she had! She went back a little and listened. Was that a noise inside, or wasn't it? She bent down and looked through the keyhole. But it was dark in the shed and she could see nothing.

But she heard something as she bent down and peeped. She heard a kind of scraping noise, she was sure she did! And then she heard a little rattling sound. After that there was silence.

'Well – I suppose it was a mouse!' she said and called down the garden to Whiskers. 'There's a mouse in here, Whiskers. You'd better come and sit by the door and scare him!' Then away she went home.

Next day Mrs Jones fed Whiskers again and petted him as she always did. He was very fond of her and rubbed himself against her legs, purring loudly.

'Well, I must go,' she said, and went back over the lawn. She suddenly remembered the noises she had heard in the shed the day before, and went close to it. And dear me, what a strange thing, she heard noises in there again!

Scrape-scrape! Rattle-rattle! And then she distinctly heard a little hissing noise.

'Bless us all – surely it can't be a snake in there!' she thought. 'No – of course not! It must have been the wind hissing through a crack. Oh, lands sake – what's that now?'

She listened. It sounded as if a lot of little things were falling down – wooden seed labels perhaps? But who was in there playing about? Could it be someone hiding in the shed?

Crash! That was quite a big noise! Mrs Jones jumped and then, feeling quite shaky, bent down and looked through the keyhole again. What had fallen down?

'Must have been a little plant-pot,' she thought, as she saw some bits and pieces on the floor of the shed. 'This is strange. Who's in there, messing about? I think I'll tell the police. Yes, I really think I will. If someone's hiding there, they may be waiting to burgle the house at night.'

So she looked out for the tall policeman whose beat was near-by, and when she saw him she went up to him.

'Excuse me, but could you just come and have a look inside the shed in the garden of Red Chimneys?' she said. 'The people are away and I feed the cat each day – and it's my belief there's someone hiding in their shed! Such noises going on – scrapings and rattling and crashings!'

'Really?' said the policeman. 'Well, I'll go and investigate right now. Come on.' So back they went to the house, and round to the shed. 'It's locked,' said the policeman, pulling at the door. 'Ah – is that a key?'

'Dear me, yes,' said Mrs Jones, staring at a big key hanging on a nail at the side of the shed. 'I never noticed that before. Well – if the key's there, and the shed's locked, there can't be anyone inside, can there?'

Crash! A noise came from the shed just as she said that, and they both jumped. 'There *is* someone there!' said the policeman. 'Come on – I'll unlock the door and go in and have a look.'

So he unlocked the door and flung it open. 'Come on out, you!' he said, sternly. 'And just tell me what you're doing there!'

But nobody came out. Not a single sound came from the shed! The policeman looked inside. It was quite a small shed and there wasn't anywhere for a person to hide. How strange!

'Nobody there, Mrs Jones,' he said, and went in at the door.

Crash! Something fell just beside him! He turned at once. A small box lay on the floor, and nails were flung around it, upset in the fall. The policeman stared at them in surprise.

'I don't like it,' said Mrs Jones, in a shaky voice. 'I really don't. Who threw that box of nails at you, Mr Policeman? There's nobody here.'

'It seemed to come from above my head,' said the policeman. 'Ah, wait – look! That little flowerpot up there is moving – down it comes! Well, I'm blessed! What is going on here? That almost hit my helmet!'

'You be careful,' said Mrs Jones. 'There's funny goings-on here. Oooh – there's that hissing again '

Sss-sss-ssss! Yes, there was certainly a hissing noise! It came from the top shelf. The policeman saw an old chair and stood on it. He looked on the crowded top shelf – and then he jumped as a small head with bright eyes peered over at him.

'What is it, what is it?' cried Mrs Jones.

'Well, bless us all – if it isn't a tortoise!' said the policeman, and he began to laugh. 'Tortoises can hiss, you know, and see, here's the box it must have been put into for its winter sleep! It woke up because the weather turned so warm, and wandered out of its box along this shelf.'

'Knocking things over!' said Mrs Jones. 'Well I never! I am sorry I called you here just for a tortoise, Mr Policeman!'

'Well, I won't arrest him!' said the policeman with a chuckle. 'And you were quite right to report to me. I'll just lock this shed and get out on my beat again.'

'No – leave it for a minute,' said Mrs Jones. 'The tortoise will want water to drink and a bit of lettuce to eat. It belongs to Peter and Julie, you know. Well, well – so you weren't a burglar hiding here, old Shelly-Back. You rascal you, tipping things down on the policeman! You wait till I tell the children of your little tricks!'

They did laugh when she told them. 'Thank you for looking after Whiskers for us,' said Julie. 'Look, we've brought back a present for you – a china cat just like Whiskers.'

'And tomorrow I shall buy you a china tortoise to go with the cat!' said Peter. 'Because you've been so kind to them both.'

Mrs Jones has them on her chimney-piece to this day – and when she told me how it was they had been given to her, I really thought I must tell you, too!

The Little Toy-Maker

The Little Toy-Maker

George and Fanny were excited because their mother had said they might go out for a picnic by themselves. 'If you cross over the road very carefully and go to the hill above the Long Field, you should be all right,' she said.

So they set off, with George carrying the picnic basket. In the basket were some egg sandwiches, two rosy apples, a small bar of chocolate, and two pieces of ginger cake. There was a bottle of lemonade as well, and George and Fanny kept thinking of the cool lemonade as they crossed the road, went through the Long Field and up the hill. They did feel so very thirsty.

There were ash and sycamore trees up on the hill. Already they were throwing down their seeds on the wind – ash spinners that spun in the breeze, and sycamore keys that twirled down to the ground. George picked some up and looked at them.

'Aren't they nice?' he said. 'Throw some up into the air, Fanny, and see them spin to the ground. The tree is pleased to see them twirling in the wind, because then it knows that its seeds are travelling far away to grow into big new trees.'

After a while the children sat down to have their lunch. They began with the egg sandwiches, but before they had taken more than a few bites they saw a most surprising sight. A very small man, not much taller than George's teddy-bear at home, came walking out from behind a gorse bush. He carried two baskets with him. One was empty and one was full. The full one had sandwiches and milk in it, and the children thought that the small man must be having a picnic, as they were.

The little man didn't see them. He had a very long white beard that he had tied neatly round his waist to keep out of the way of his feet. He wore enormous glasses on his big nose, and he had funny pointed ears and a hat that had tiny bells on. The bells tinkled as he walked. Fanny wished and wished that she had a hat like that.

'What a very little man!' said Fanny. 'Do you suppose he is a pixie or a brownie?'

'Shh!' said George. 'Don't talk. Let's watch.'

So they watched. The little man walked along humming a song – and suddenly he tripped over a root and down he went! His full basket tipped up, and out fell his sandwiches and milk. The bottle broke. The sandwiches split open and fell into bits on the grass.

'Oh! What a pity!' cried George, and ran to help at once. The little man was surprised to see him. George picked him up, brushed the grass off his clothes, and looked sadly at the milk and sandwiches.

'Your picnic is no use,' he said. 'Come and share ours. Do!'

The small man smiled and his face lit up at once. He picked up his baskets and went to where the children had spread their picnic food. Soon he was sitting down chatting to them, sharing their sandwiches, cake, and chocolate. He was very pleased.

'Why was one of your baskets empty?' asked Fanny. 'What were you going to put into it?'

'Ash and sycamore keys,' said the small man. 'There are plenty on this hill.'

'Shall we help you to fill your basket?' said George. 'We've eaten everything now and Fanny and I would like to help you.'

'Oh, do,' said the small man. So the three of them picked up the ash and sycamore keys, and put them neatly into the basket.

'Why do you collect these?' asked Fanny. 'I would so like to know. Do you burn them, or something?'

'Oh no. I'm a toy-maker and I use them for keys for

my clockwork toys,' said the little man. 'Come along home with me, if you like. I'll show you what I do.'

He took them over the top of the hill and there, under a mossy curtain, was a tiny green door set in the side of the hill. The little man pushed a sycamore key into the door and unlocked it. Inside was a tiny room, set with small furniture and a big work-table.

And on the table were all kinds of toys! They were made out of hazelnut shells, acorns, chestnuts, pine cones, and all sorts of things! The small man had cleverly made bodies and heads and legs and wings, and there were the toys, very small, but very quaint and beautiful. The children stared at them in delight.

'Now, you see,' said the little man, emptying out his basket of keys on to his work-table, 'now, you see, all I need to do is to find keys to fit these toys, and then they can be wound up and they will walk and run and dance. Just fit a few keys into the holes and see if you can wind up any of the toys.'

In great excitement the two children fitted ash and

sycamore keys into the toys, and George found one that fitted a pine-cone bird perfectly. He wound it up – and the bird danced and hopped, pecked and even flapped its funny wings. It was lovely to watch.

Soon all the funny little toys were dancing about on the table, and the children clapped their hands in joy. It was the funniest sight they had ever seen! They only had to fit a key to any of the toys, wind it up – and lo and behold, that toy came to life!

'I wish we hadn't got to go, but we must. Mum will be worried if we're late,' said George at last. 'Goodbye, little fellow. I do love your toys.'

'Choose one each,' said the little man generously. So they did. Fanny chose the bird and George chose a hedgehog made very cleverly out of a prickly chestnut-case and a piece of beech-mast. It ran just like a real hedgehog when George wound it up.

And now those two little toys are on their mantelpiece at home, and they are so funny to watch when George and Fanny wind them up with ash or sycamore keys. I can't show you the toys – but you can go and find ash and sycamore keys for yourself if you like. There are plenty under the trees, spinning in the wind. Find a few, and see what good little keys they make for winding up fairy toys!

Billy's Bicycle

Billy's Bicycle

Billy had a bicycle. It had belonged to his brother, and when John had grown too big for it he had put it into the shed and left it there all by itself. John had had a new one, and so the old bicycle had lain there, rusty and forgotten.

When Billy grew big enough for a bicycle he remembered John's. 'Oh, I wonder if it would do for me, or if it is too broken and old!' he thought.

So he went to have a look at it. There it was in the shed, leaning against the seed-boxes and the barrel of oil.

Billy looked at it. 'I like the look of you,' he said to

the bicycle. 'You certainly look old, but you look nice and friendly somehow – as if you'd like me to ride on you.'

Now this was just exactly what the bicycle was feeling! It badly wanted Billy to ride it. It liked the look of him very much, for Billy was one of those smiley children that everyone likes.

Billy took the bicycle out into the garden. 'My goodness, you are rusty!' he said. 'Your paint is all worn off and your bell is broken – it won't ring. I don't think much of you at the moment, but I do believe I could make you quite smart again if I get a pot of paint, and if I rub the rust off your bright parts.'

The bicycle was thrilled to hear this. It is dreadful to be old, rusty and dirty – and simply lovely to hear somebody say that they can make you look fine again. The bicycle wished it had a bell to ring. It felt quite sure it would have rung it for joy, if it had!

Well, Billy was as good as his word. He spent some money on a pot of black paint and a pot of red paint.

He painted that bicycle till it looked as new as could be. He rubbed away the rust, and made the bright parts shine.

'I'll buy a new bell for you and a new saddlebag,' said Billy. 'I'll have your brakes put right too. And there's a screw gone at the back. I'll get that put right. And I'll pump up your tyres and ride you! You and I will have some fine times together, bike!'

Well, in a week's time that bicycle was just like a new one. It shone beautifully, and its new bell rang as loudly as could be! Its tyres were nice and hard, and spun along the road joyfully.

The old bicycle was very happy. It loved to feel Billy on its saddle, pedalling away hard. It helped him all it could. It tried not to run over big stones. It tried not to go into puddles and splash him.

They had some good times together, Billy and the bike. They went everywhere – to school, to the park, to the hills, and to the woods. The bicycle enjoyed itself tremendously. It had been so lonely and sad lying in the dark shed by itself.

Now it could talk to other bicycles and cars and could have its bell rung at corners so that it felt most important! Ah, this was the kind of life for a bicycle!

Billy kept his bicycle beautifully. He cleaned it well. He kept the bright parts shining. He oiled it and pumped up the tyres properly. He didn't fling it down on the ground as other boys did with their bicycles. And the old bike loved him for it, and sang a little purring song as it went along the road.

'I wish I could do something for Billy!' it sang. 'Billy's done plenty for me! I wish I could do something for Billy! Billy's done plenty for me!'

Now one evening, when the bicycle was leaning against the shed, waiting for Billy to come out and put it away, it was surprised to see a boy's head peeping just over the fence.

'What's that boy doing?' thought the bicycle in surprise. 'Why is he peeping all round like that? This is very strange.'

The boy saw that nobody was about. He jumped over the fence and ran to the apple-shed in which were stored all the cooking and eating apples. My word, that boy was going to have a feast!

The bicycle watched him go into the apple-shed. He heard him munching apples. He saw him filling a sack with them. And the bicycle was very angry!

'Billy's mother may think that Billy took those apples!' it said. It wondered what to do. It couldn't ride off by itself and warn Billy. But it could ring its bell!

So it rang it. *R-r-r-r-ring, r-r-r-r-ring, r-r-r-r-ring! R-r r ring!*

The boy in the shed was alarmed. He put his head out to see what was happening. He didn't for one moment think that it was the bicycle bell ringing!

But he saw the bicycle and an idea came into his head. He could ride it away quickly and nobody would catch him!

He put the sack of apples over his shoulder, ran to

the bicycle, jumped on it and rode it away. The bicycle rang its bell in despair:

R-r-r-ring! R-r-r-ring! R-r-r-ring!

But Billy was out with his father and couldn't hear it. So out of the gate the bike had to go, with the bad boy riding it. How it hated it! But it couldn't help itself, for when its pedals were pushed round and round it just had to go!

And then, coming down the street, the bicycle saw Billy and his father! They were going home. The bicycle was so excited. Now perhaps Billy would see it!

But Billy was looking into the shops as he passed and he didn't notice his bicycle. So the bicycle rang its bell desperately again:

R-r-r-r-ring! R-r-r-ring! R-r-r-r-ring!

Billy looked round. He knew the sound of that bicycle bell. He stared hard at the bicycle as it went by. Could it possibly be his? No – surely it couldn't!

The bicycle saw a big stone in its way. It ran at it,

and wobbled over it. The bad boy tried to balance himself, but he couldn't, because the bicycle wobbled so. Down he fell with a crash and the apples flew all over the road!

Billy and his father went to help him up. The bicycle rang its bell again:

R-r-r-ring! R-r-r-ring! R-r-r-ring!

Then Billy looked closely at the bicycle and he knew that it was his. What an extraordinary thing!

'What are you doing on my bicycle?' he asked the boy. 'You bad boy – and I think those are our apples too!'

The boy began to cry. He had hurt his knee very badly, and he was frightened, for he knew that he had done very wrong. He confessed all that he had done, and Billy's father looked very stern.

'You will come back to our house and I will bind up your knee,' he said. 'Then I shall take you back to your own home and speak to your father about you. I think you need to have a good punishment, and I shall see that you get it. How dare you come to my apple-shed, steal my apples, and ride off on my son's bicycle! It's a good thing you rang the bell when you did, or Billy wouldn't have heard it and looked round.'

'I didn't ring the bell,' said the boy, wiping his eyes with a very dirty hand. 'It seemed to ring all by itself. It was very strange.'

'Bells don't ring by themselves,' said Billy's father. But he was wrong, wasn't he! And just to show that he was, the bicycle rang its bell again, very softly and happily:

R-r-r-ring! R-r-r-ring! R-r-r-r-ring! I've done something for Billy at last! R-r-r-ring! R-r-r-ring! R-r-r-r-ring!

That Girl
Next Door!

That Girl Next Door!

Dick, Juliet and Robert loved the girl next door, but their mother didn't.

'I never knew such a tomboy!' she said. 'Always climbing trees and tearing her clothes and shouting and playing cowboys and Indians and goodness knows what!'

'But, Mum, she's fun,' said Dick. 'Anyway, she hasn't got a mother to tell her not to, poor thing.'

'Tessa's nice,' said Juliet. 'She's kind.'

'I like playing with her,' said Robert.

'Well – I suppose there's no harm in her,' said their mother. 'But she is so noisy! And she always looks such a little mess. Still, having no mother does make things difficult. She's got no one to teach her to be clean and good mannered.'

The three children lived near the wide River Thames. Their father had a boat but he wouldn't let them go in it unless he was there. For one thing his children couldn't swim, and he was afraid they might fall into the water.

Tessa could swim like a fish. She said she had taught herself. She could row a boat, too, though her father hadn't got one of his own. In fact, or so the children thought, Tessa could do anything!

One day the children's mother had to go and see her sister, who was ill.

'Now I shall have to leave you three alone for a little while,' she said. 'I hope that girl next door doesn't come in and lead you into mischief. But I think she's out. Now, just be good children while I'm gone.'

And off she went. She hadn't been gone for more

than five minutes when Tessa came to the fence and gave her loud call. 'Coo-eeee!'

'It's Tessa!' said the three children and ran eagerly into the garden.

'Hello,' said Tessa. 'Shall we play? Will your mother mind if I come into your garden?'

'She's out,' said Dick. 'Come in, Tessa. We can play one of your "let's pretend" games.'

'Ooooh, yes,' said Juliet and Robert. Tessa was marvellous at 'let's pretend'. She could be a most lifelike cowboy, or shipwrecked sailor, or pirate or policeman or burglar. It really was exciting when she played.

'I know what we'll play today,' said Tessa, climbing over the wall. 'Let's play shipwrecked sailors.'

'Oh, yes. How do you play it?' said Juliet.

'Well, we want a desert island to be wrecked on – that round bit of grass will do,' said Tessa, and the bit of grass immediately looked like a desert island. 'And we want a raft to get away on.'

'A raft?' echoed the others. 'How can we make a raft?'

Tessa knew how to make a raft, of course. 'You know that old kitchen table of yours?' she said. 'Well, that will make a wonderful raft – upside down, you know, with a white flag flying from one of the legs as a signal to our rescuers.'

This all sounded very exciting – but Dick didn't know whether his mother would like them to use her old kitchen table. 'Oh, don't be silly,' said Tessa, 'we're not going to damage it! I'll help you to bring it out.'

Well, it wasn't long before the game was going well. They were all truly shipwrecked on the desert island – and then Tessa pretended to build the raft. She even borrowed a hammer from the toolbox and hammered at the raft as if she really was making it. Everything she did was so real.

'Now we must tie a flag to one of the legs,' she said. 'What about that white cloth on your line? That's just the right size.'

The white cloth was tied to the leg.

'Now we want a paddle,' said Tessa. 'Get one of your spades – the biggest one. I'll do the paddling. What a pity this is all pretence! If only we could float away on the river!'

It was a lovely game. They all got on the upside-down table and Tessa paddled valiantly, telling them to keep their eyes open for a rescue boat. It was when Juliet was shading her eyes, looking for a rescue boat, that she suddenly saw something that frightened her.

'Tessa – stop! I saw somebody falling in the river,' she said, clutching Tessa's arm. 'You know that little boy who lives on the other side of the river? It was him. I'm sure it was!'

They all gazed over the river. Then they heard a scream. They saw something being washed into midstream, and the three children were in a panic.

But not Tessa. She knew what to do at once. She jumped out of the table-raft and yelled to the others. 'Help me to carry it to the river, come on, quick! This is as good as a boat. I'll go after the little boy.'

The children were too dazed not to obey. They half-ran with the upside-down table through the gate to the river, and Tessa launched it on the water, jumping in herself with the little spade for a paddle.

The table was wood and floated well. Tessa began to paddle fast with the little spade, her eyes on the bundle of clothes that was the little boy from across the river. That was all he looked like as he floated along – just a bunch of clothes.

The current was taking him out to midstream. Tessa paddled manfully. She got nearer and nearer. The boy bobbed close, and she sat down, clutched a table leg and grabbed at the boy's shirt as he bobbed nearer still. She got hold of him!

But she couldn't pull him on the table-raft because every time she tried the table almost turned over. Tessa wondered what to do. Then she saw that a boat was coming swiftly near. Someone else had seen what had happened.

A man dived in and came up near the child. He took him from Tessa and life-saved him, swimming strongly with the child's face uppermost. Willing hands dragged them both aboard the little boat and rowed back to the child's home on the opposite side.

'Well done, thank you!' a voice called to her from the boat. Tessa waved and then paddled her raft back to shore. And there, on the bank, was the children's mother, home from her visit! The children had told her what was happening, and she was waiting there for Tessa.

'Oh dear!' thought Tessa. 'Now I shall get into trouble for taking the table out on the water!'

But she didn't! The children's mother kissed her and praised her. 'You saved that boy's life!' she said. 'You're a fine girl, Tessa. How proud your mother would have been of you. Now don't look as if I'm going to scold you for going off with my table – I'm not. Shall we make a bargain, Tessa?'

'What bargain?' asked Tessa, slipping her hand

into the hand of the children's mother.

'You let me teach you how to sew and speak nicely and learn good manners as Dick, Juliet and Robert do,' said their mother. 'And in return will you teach my three how to swim and how to row and run and jump like you do?'

'Will you be like a mother?' asked Tessa, delighted. 'I always wanted a real mother.'

'I will,' said the children's mother. 'I'll have four children instead of three! And now come along and have a very special tea on that wonderful old kitchen table. Little did it know it was to be a raft some day and go floating on the water!'

When the other three can swim they're planning to go out on that table together. I only hope it will bear their weight – but still, as Tessa says, what does it matter if it sinks? They'll simply be shipwrecked sailors swimming to the shore!

The Boy Who Never Put Things Back

The Boy Who Never Put Things Back

Did you ever know a boy called George, who could never remember to put things back into their places? Well, this is a story about him.

George was about ten years old, and he had two brothers and two sisters, all older than he was. They were fond of George, although they often called him the baby of the family, which he didn't like at all. He was always trying to be big and grown-up, so that his brothers and sisters would take him about with them and let him join in their games.

'I don't like being left out of things just because I'm the youngest,' he said to his mother. 'It's not fair. I can't help being the youngest.'

'There's no need for you to be left out,' his mother said. 'Behave yourself, be kind to the others, do odd jobs for them when you can, and you will see they will take you out on picnics with them.'

There was one thing that George was always getting into trouble for – and that was, he never would put things back into their places! Do you know anyone like that? They are really most annoying people.

George used to like cutting out from papers and magazines, but he had no scissors of his own. So what did he do but go to his big sister Mary's work basket and borrow her scissors. But when he had finished cutting out, he wouldn't put the scissors back again! No, he would leave them on the table, and then someone would clear them away.

When Mary wanted them, they wouldn't be in her work basket, and then she would spend half an hour hunting for them. That would make her very cross.

'I don't mind you borrowing my things, but you

might at least have the decency to put them back!' she would say to George.

Then he would borrow Alec's pencil and leave it lying somewhere in the garden. Or he would go off with Mother's pen to write a letter and not take it back. She would find it in his pocket a week later, when she had given up looking for it.

His mother and all his older brothers and sisters scolded him well for this silly habit, but although George kept promising to be better, he wasn't. He was too lazy-minded to try and remember to take borrowed things back.

Now one summer everyone was in a great state of excitement because they were going to the seaside. The older children were going to ride down on their bicycles, picnic on the way, spend a night at a camp, and then join the rest of the family at the hotel next day.

George listened to all the arrangements being made. When he heard that only the four older ones were to ride down to the sea and he was to go by train the next day, he was angry and hurt.

'Mother! Why can't *I* go with the others? I'm ten, aren't I? Why can't I ride with them? I've got a lovely new bicycle, I'm a very good rider, and I want to go with the others.'

'Don't talk like that to me, George,' said his mother. 'That's not the way to get anything you want. You wouldn't be able to ride so far.'

'Oh, Mother, I could, I could!' said George, and he put his arms round his mother to coax her. 'Let me, please. Ask Alec if I can't ride well now! Ask Mary! I went all the way to the woods and back with her last week. Oh, do, do let me. I can't tell you how much I want to ride off with the others, and sleep in a camp for the night. I don't want to be a baby and go by train.'

'I should think you could let him come with us, Mother,' said Alec. 'He's good on his bike. I'll look after him. It would be nice for him to have his bike by the sea too, because then he could come for rides and picnics with us. Otherwise he won't be able to.'

They all talked it over, and to George's enormous delight Mother at last decided to let him ride off with the others. How simply marvellous!

'I shall feel so big,' thought George, as he polished up his bicycle the next day. 'Fancy going off all by ourselves – and sleeping in a camp for the night!'

The bicycles were kept in two sheds. Alec's, Mary's, Peter's and Jane's went in one shed, and George's, his mother's and his father's went in the other. They were all good bicycles, and their father insisted that they should be well looked after and cleaned each week.

The children thought the day would never come for them to start off. But at last the day before came, and they all took out their bicycles for a last polish and to make sure they had no punctures. They put them back into the sheds, shut the doors and went to help their mother with the last-minute packing.

George was having a friend to tea. It was Penny, the little girl from next door. She collected stamps and so did George. They had five stamp albums each, and they went to tea with one another once a week to swap stamps, stick them into their albums and gloat over their collections.

After tea the two of them took out their stamp albums. Penny bent over hers – and then she sat up with a cry. A spot of red had fallen on to her precious album!

'Oh, George – my nose is bleeding again! I shall have to sit with my head back till it stops. Wipe that spot carefully off the page for me.'

'Bother!' said George, looking at Penny. Her nose often bled and it was such a nuisance because then she had to stop whatever she was doing.

'Mother's busy,' said George, 'or I'd fetch her.'

'It's all right,' said Penny, mopping her nose. 'It'll soon stop. It never lasts long.'

But it did seem to last a long time. Penny lay down on her back on the floor to try and stop it. But it still didn't.

'We're wasting all this time,' said George. 'Is there anything else to do for nose-bleeding besides lying on the floor?'

'Well, once Granny put the biggest key she had down my back,' said Penny. 'She said that would stop it.'

'What a funny idea!' said George. 'Shall we try it? I know where there is a very big key.'

'All right. Fetch it,' said poor Penny. 'You can stick it down my back and perhaps the coldness will stop the bleeding.'

George sped off to the bicycle shed where his bike was kept. There was a very big key in the lock there. He took it out and ran back. He pushed it down Penny's back. She squealed.

'Oooh! It's terribly cold. Oooh, it makes me wriggle!'

But very soon the nose-bleeding stopped and she could sit up. 'I don't know if it was the key or whether it was really going to stop,' she said. 'Anyway, I'm better now. Let's get on with our stamps.'

So they got on with their stamps and had a fine time swapping and arranging. Then it was time for Penny to go.

'Goodbye,' she said. 'Come to tea with me as soon as you get back. I hope you have a fine holiday.'

'I'm biking down with the others!' said George grandly. 'Going to spend a night at a camp! It'll be fine.'

The next day came. The children were to set off at ten o'clock. They had their few night things with them in kit-bags, and their packages of food. Mother gave George his, too. He did feel proud.

'Now get your bikes, and I'll come to the front gate to see you off,' she said. 'Take care of George, Peter.'

They all went to get their bikes. Alec, Mary, Peter and Jane wheeled theirs out of the shed. But George couldn't get his.

'The other shed's locked,' he said. 'I can't get my bike.'

'Well, unlock it, silly!' called Alec. 'Can't you turn the key?'

'It's not here,' said George, and he rattled the door.

Mother came up. 'What's the matter? Don't shake the door like that.'

'Mother, the key's gone. I can't get my bike,' said George in a panic.

'Well, where *is* the key?' said Mother. 'It can't be far away. Has anyone taken it?'

'Oh!' said George, remembering suddenly. 'Yes, I took it! Penny's nose bled yesterday, and I borrowed the key to put down her back. It must be in the playroom.' He sped off to get it. He hunted everywhere for it. It didn't seem to be anywhere at all. Alec yelled up to him.

'Oh, do come on, George. It's quarter-past ten. We shall never get to camp tonight if we start late now.'

'Oh, wait for me, wait for me!' cried poor George, tearing about the room and hunting for the key. Mother came up and helped him.

'George, I don't know how many times I've told you to put things back when you've borrowed them,' she said. 'Now you see what's happened! You're making everybody late.'

'Let's try the key of the other shed,' said Mary. So they did, but it didn't fit.

'Well, we can't wait any more,' said Peter at half-past ten. 'We must go. George must come with you by train, Mother.'

'Oh no, oh no! Wait for me! Don't go without me!' begged George. 'Oh, I couldn't bear it. Mother, can't we break open the door to get my bike?'

'Certainly not,' said Mother. 'Now, George, this is entirely your own fault. You will have to put up with the results of your silliness. You took the key and you should have put it back. You didn't, so we can't get your bike. The others are not going to wait, so you will have to go with us tomorrow.'

And that is just what happened. The others mounted their bicycles, waved goodbye and set off – without poor George. He was ten, and a big boy, but he was so bitterly disappointed that he went to the bottom of the garden and cried by himself for a whole hour.

Daddy was not very comforting that night when he heard about it. 'Well, sooner or later I knew that silly habit of yours of taking things and never putting them back would bring you a good punishment,' he said. 'It's a pity, George – but if you do things like that you must expect things to go wrong.'

'I wish I knew where the key was!' said George. 'Oh, Mother – if I don't find it I suppose I can't take my bike away on the train?'

'You certainly can't,' said Mother. So George spent the whole evening hunting for that key, but he couldn't find it. He had to go to bed very sad indeed.

The next day Mother, Daddy and George got ready for the train. Just about ten minutes before the taxi-cab came, Penny came running up.

'George! Did you want the key you put down my

back yesterday? I went home with it still down my back, but I thought I had better bring it to you this morning in case it was important.'

'Oh, Penny! You horrid, horrid girl! You went off with the key! Now I haven't been able to go with the others,' said George, and he almost slapped Penny.

'Stop that, George!' said his father at once. 'It was you who should have thought of the key and taken it back, not Penny. I won't have you blaming anyone else. That's a coward's trick. Take the blame yourself, as you should, and act properly.'

'Sorry, Penny,' said George, feeling really ashamed. His father nodded to his mother.

'Well, as George seems to be sorry, he can take his bike with him. There's just time to get it before the taxi comes. He can bring it on the train with him.'

George sped off with the key. He got out his bike. Now at least he would be able to go for rides with the others. But oh, what a pity he hadn't been able to go with them the day before! That would have been such a wonderful treat!

'I shall always put things back in future,' thought George. 'I gave myself a terrible disappointment by forgetting about the key. I won't let things like this happen again.'

Did you guess where the key was? You are clever if you did!

Policeman Billy

Policeman Billy

There was once a small boy called Billy, who loved dressing up. One birthday he was very pleased because his Uncle Jim gave him a set of policeman's clothes! They were just big enough for him. There was a blue tunic, a belt and a fine plastic helmet which looked just like the one a real policeman would have.

'Ooh!' said Billy in delight. 'Just exactly what I wanted! Now I can dress up and pretend to be a policeman!'

'Here's a pencil and a notebook for you,' said his father. 'If you're going to be a policeman you must have those. You can write down things about the people you see then. You never know when your notes will come in useful!'

Billy was so pleased. He was soon dressed in his policeman's uniform, and very smart he looked, I can tell you! It was a pity there were no trousers to go with it, because Billy felt that his shorts didn't look exactly right with the uniform – but that couldn't be helped!

'I will pretend there are robbers up on the common,' said Billy to his mother. 'I am going up there with my notebook. I'll hide under a bush and make notes about all the people going by, in case they happen to be my pretend robbers!'

His mother laughed, 'Run along, then!' she said. 'I hope you'll be a successful policeman!'

Billy ran off, proud to be dressed in a policeman's blue uniform, helmet and all! He had his notebook and pencil in his pocket. What a fine game he was going to have!

He was soon up on the common. It was a fine day

and the sun shone down hotly. Billy found a bush and sat underneath it, waiting for people to come by, for the road was quite near. But very soon he felt too hot. His helmet seemed very heavy, but he couldn't bear to take it off. Besides, he was quite sure that a real policeman would have to keep it on.

Not far off was a little broken-down shed. Billy thought he would go and hide there. It would be cooler in the shed than outside on the common. He could easily peep through a crack in the wooden walls and see who passed by.

He ran to the shed. It was very dark inside, for the only window was very small indeed, and it was so dirty that hardly any light came through at all. At one end of the shed there was a crack in the wooden wall, and Billy sat down on some sacks and put his eye to the crack. He could see the road quite well from there. He took out his notebook. He could only just see to write in it! He put the date, and the place where he was, and then he began to wait patiently.

Soon Mr Straws the farmer came by on his tractor. Billy wrote down: *At a quarter past 10 saw Mr Straws on his tractor, wearing old brown jacket and no cap.* After that Mrs Lane went by on her bicycle. Billy entered her into his book too: *At half past 10 Mrs Lane went by on bicycle, wearing blue skirt, blue jumper and black hat. She had a big hole in the back of her right stocking.*

'I would make a good real policeman, I'm sure,' thought Billy to himself, as he wrote. 'I do notice things. Daddy says that's one of the first things a policeman learns to do – to notice even little things.'

After that no one came by for a long time. Billy felt sleepy. It was fun to be a policeman, but a bit boring when nothing much happened. Also it was rather smelly in the shed.

Then he heard the noise of a car. He put his eye to the crack and looked through. He saw that a dark blue car was coming slowly along. The man at the wheel was alone. He seemed to be looking out for something. Just as Billy was writing down: *At 1/4 past 11 a dark blue saloon car came by, number GHR 419, with one man . . .* the car stopped. Billy peeped again. The man looked quickly all round him and then took a bundle out of the car. He ran swiftly over the common to the shed where Billy was. But he didn't go inside. He went to the back of it where he could not be seen from the road. Billy was astonished. He sat still for a minute and wondered what to do. What would a real policeman do? Well, a real policeman would find out what the man was doing and put it all down, he was sure. Billy got up and went to the other side of the shed to find a crack that he could look through. He soon found one and peeped out.

The man was there – and he was behaving very strangely! He had taken off his coat and shirt and was busy putting on a brown jersey, and a brown coat over that! He threw his cap into a bush and put on a hat instead. Then he did something very peculiar indeed! He took a little black thing out of a pocket and stuck it firmly on his top lip.

'Gosh, he's given himself a moustache!' thought Billy, amazed. 'Whatever can he be doing all that for? Is he playing a game of pretend like me? Well I'd better write all this down, I think. It's very exciting.'

So he wrote in his notebook: *The man hid at back of shed, and changed his clothes. He threw his old clothes into a big gorse bush nearby. He put on a brown jersey and a brown coat, and grey hat. He also put on a little black moustache. The man was small and had one of his thumbs bandaged up. His nose was a bit crooked. I couldn't see the colour of his eyes, but his hair was red-brown.*

The man looked all round him once more, saw that no one was coming and ran back to his car. He jumped into it and off he went at top speed. Billy wrote again in his notebook: *The man got into the car and drove off fast towards Winter Hill.*

After that nobody else came at all for a whole hour. It was very boring. Billy nearly went to sleep. He did wish something else exciting would happen, like that man who came and changed his clothes.

Suddenly Billy saw two real policemen driving slowly up the road, in a police car. They stopped not far off, got out of the car and sat down on a seat by the side of the road. Billy thought he would go and talk to them. Whatever would they say when they saw a small, dressed-up policeman like himself! He ran out of the shed and went up to them immediately.

'Hello, who's this!' said one of the policemen, with a grin. 'Good morning, Inspector!'

'Good morning, sir!' said the other policeman taking out his notebook and pretending to look through it very solemnly, shaking his head. 'What about you, Inspector?' he said to Billy, shutting his notebook with a snap. 'Have you anything to report? Or perhaps you don't keep a notebook?'

'Of course I do!' said Billy indignantly. 'And I'd say mine's a nicer notebook than yours, too! I've written quite a lot in it this morning.'

'Let me see,' said the first policeman grinning, and he held out his hand. Billy gave him the notebook and the policeman turned over the pages, reading all about Mr Straws going by in his tractor, and about Mrs Lane and the hole in her stocking.

But when he came to the big piece about the man in the car, the policeman stopped smiling. He read it all through very carefully, and then passed the book over to his companion.

'Read that!' he said. 'What do you make of it?' Then he turned to Billy. 'Did you make all that up?' he asked. 'Or did it really happen?'

'Of course it happened!' said Billy. 'I can show you where the old clothes are, in a big gorse bush.'

Both policemen sprang to their feet. Billy showed them where the man had thrown the clothes, and they pulled them out quickly.

'Good grief, it must have been Sid Brown who pulled off the robbery last night!' said the first policeman. 'We must go back to the station, Ted. We'll catch him now we know what he's dressed like – a moustache and all, too – and a bandaged thumb!

We'll soon have him! Come on, sonny, jump in the back of the car and we'll take you with us!'

So, still dressed in his policeman's uniform, Billy, tremendously excited, rode in the back of the police car all the way to the police station. There they saw a real inspector, who solemnly read Billy's notebook, gave a lot of sharp orders, asked Billy a good many questions and then made a lot of phone calls.

It was near Billy's lunch-time and he felt hungry. 'Could I go home now?' he asked. 'My mother will be wondering where I am.'

'Yes, you can go off duty, Inspector!' said the real inspector, beaming at Billy. 'You've done well today, young man – we shall catch a thief who's been worrying us for a long time!'

Billy tore off in delight. But when he got home and told his mother and father they laughed at him.

'You're making it all up, Billy!' said his mother and they simply would not believe him when he said it was all quite true – he had seen the man, he had seen the policemen, he had been to the police station, and he had helped to catch a real thief!

But his parents soon changed their minds when a big policeman came to the house that evening and told them that, thanks to Billy's notebook, they had managed to catch Sid Brown, the clever thief! How pleased and proud they were!

'So you *were* a real policeman today!' said his mother, hugging him. 'And not a pretend one!'

The next week a parcel came for Billy. Inside was – what do you think? A fine policeman's whistle, and a policeman's waterproof cape, made just the right size! The note with it said: *For Chief Inspector Billy – with compliments from Chief Inspector Rawlings.*

Wasn't Billy proud! Well – you should just see him all dressed up now, cape, whistle and all, just like a real policeman!

Think Hard, Boatman

Think Hard, Boatman

Splash, the ferryman, lived in a tiny house beside the river. He had a cheerful-looking little boat painted blue and the oars were orange. The boat was called *Here-we-go!* and everyone liked going across the river in it.

Splash was really a very busy little man. He took the postman across to deliver letters to the farms on the other side of the water. He took old Mrs Dumble to and fro every day when she went shopping. He took four children over and back each day too, because they went to Dame Little's School up the hill.

He sang as he rowed his boat to and fro:

Over the river and back I go,
My little bright oars a-flashing,
Watch me ferrying to and fro,

Here-we-go, here-we-go, splashing!

When he sang the word 'splashing' he dashed the oars hard into the water and made a terrific splash. Everyone liked that very much except old Mrs Dumble, who said that it made her jump and wetted her shawl.

Splash never refused to take anyone. Even when Mighty-One the wizard came, he didn't say no, though he shivered and shook all the time in case the wizard might suddenly work a spell and take the boat off to the moon, or some other peculiar place.

And when Fat-One, the giant, wanted to be rowed across the river, even then Splash didn't say no! But he was so afraid the giant would weigh down the boat too much at his end that he put a big stone just beside his own seat, so that the boat wouldn't tip too much.

It made the rowing very hard, because the boat was heavy then, with the giant and the stone. Still, somehow Splash managed, and he made it quite a boast that he had never said no to anyone who wanted to go across the river, or wanted goods rowed across to the other side.

But wait a minute! There was a time when Splash very nearly *did* say no! It was when old Witch Grim told him she was going to leave him some goods to take across for her. Splash didn't know what the goods were, but he didn't like the sound of them.

'You've got to be careful with my goods,' the witch said. 'If any get damaged I shall make you pay, Splash. In fact, I might even take your boat away!'

'When will you leave the goods to be taken across?' asked Splash. 'And what are they?'

'Two animals and a nice big bag of carrots,' said Witch Grim. 'Mr Quick will bring them in his cart this evening.'

Well, when Mr Quick came with his cart, Splash happened to be the other side of the river with old Mrs Dumble. Mr Quick hailed him loudly.

'Hey, Splash! Here are the goods from Witch Grim. I can't wait, so hurry up and fetch them before they damage one another.'

Splash rowed back as fast as he could, and there, waiting for him on the other side, were the goods.

One red fox, all alive-oh!

One white rabbit, scared of the fox.

One bag of carrots that made the rabbit feel very hungry indeed.

'Well now!' said Splash, scratching his head and looking at the goods. 'I can't possibly take more than one of you across at once. You'd be too heavy for me, because I'm tired now. Which shall I take first?'

'Take me!' said the rabbit. 'I'm scared of the fox. Take me, Mr Splash, and leave me safely on the other side. Then row back and get the carrots.'

'Right,' said Splash. Then he stopped and scratched

his head again. 'Ah, but wait a minute! If I take you across – and then fetch the bag of carrots and leave it with you, you'll nibble the lot! I know you, Rabbit!'

'Well, take the rabbit across, and then take me, and take the carrots last,' said the fox.

'Right,' said the boatman. But the rabbit gave a loud squeal.

'Oh, no Mr Splash! If you do that you will have to leave the fox alone with me on the other side whilst you go back for the carrots – and he'll eat me!'

'Take me across first then,' said the fox.

'Aha – and leave the carrots and the rabbit together on this side!' said Splash. 'Not if I know it, Red Fox!'

'Well, what are you going to do then?' said the red fox. 'Either the rabbit and I are left together on one side or the other, or the rabbit and the carrots.'

Splash sat down on a tree-stump and scratched his head again. He thought very hard indeed. He simply must not leave rabbit and fox together, or rabbit and carrots. The fox would eat the rabbit, the rabbit would eat the carrots – and then Witch Grim would be very angry and take his boat away.

The red fox sat down too and grinned at Splash. 'It's no good,' he said. 'Work it out how you will, Splash, *something's* going to be eaten. And *you're* going to get into trouble!'

Think hard, boatman! Think hard! There's a way to do it, if only you'll think hard.

What, you don't think there is? Think again. Yes, Splash, you can do it, and nothing will be eaten, but just think hard and find out how!

Splash thought so hard that his eyes disappeared under an enormous frown. Then he jumped up and smacked his hands together loudly. The fox and rabbit jumped.

'I know how to do it!' said Splash.

'You don't,' said the fox, disappointed.

'I do!' said Splash. 'Rabbit, get into the boat! You're the first to go across.'

The rabbit got in, looking very doubtful. Splash

rowed him across to the other side and left him there. He rowed back to where he had left the fox and the carrots. He popped the carrots into his boat and rowed back to the rabbit.

'Hey!' called the fox. 'The rabbit will eat the carrots if you leave them over there with him.'

But Splash didn't mean to do that. Oh no! he threw out the bag of carrots and called to the surprised rabbit to get back into the boat again – and he rowed him back to the fox!

'Now get out,' he said to the rabbit, 'and you, Red Fox, get in! I'm leaving you on this side again for a bit, Rabbit. I'll be back to fetch you soon.'

He rowed the fox across to where he had left the carrots and made him get out. 'The carrots will be safe enough with *you!*' he said. 'Now I'm off to get the rabbit!'

And back he went to get the rabbit. He rowed him over to the fox and the carrots. 'There!' he said. 'I've done it – and nothing's eaten! And here comes

Witch Grim to fetch you all! Hey, Witch Grim, my fee, please!'

'What! You managed to get these goods across safely!' said Witch Grim. 'Splash, you're very, very clever. I quite expected either the rabbit or the carrots would be eaten!'

Splash *was* clever, wasn't he? Would *you* have thought of that way, do you think?

The Wishing Spells

The Wishing Spells

'Are you going to take those boots and shoes out this morning?' Ma called to little Shuffle. 'Well, then, will you deliver these three wishing spells to Dame Dandy for me?'

'Right, Ma,' said Shuffle. He put the mended boots and shoes into a basket and set off, whistling. The wishing spells were in a little yellow packet on the top of the boots. Shuffle kept looking down at it to make sure it was still there.

'Can't lose wishing spells,' thought little Shuffle. 'Very dangerous if they got into the hands of the wrong people.'

Now, as he went through the wood, along came Grabbit the gnome, and with him was his sister, Mrs Well-I-Never. They both stopped at once.

'Well, I never! There's little Shuffle large as life and twice as natural,' said Mrs Well-I-Never.

'Being a good boy and taking back all his mended boots and shoes,' said Grabbit. 'And how are all your mother's cats, Shuffle?'

Shuffle didn't like this. He began to edge away. They came closer, and Mrs Well-I-Never's sharp eyes caught sight of the little yellow packet on top of the basket.

'Well, I never! If that isn't one of Ma Shuffle's packets of spells. Let me see, Shuffle.' And before little Shuffle could stop her she had snatched the yellow packet and opened it. Out came the three tiny wishing spells.

Mrs Well-I-Never knew what they were at once. 'Grabbit,' she said, giving them to her brother, 'look here, wishing spells! We've never had any in our lives.'

'Give them back,' said Shuffle, feeling very uncomfortable indeed. 'They won't do you any good. Ma says however much people like you are given good things like wishing spells, you'll only get bad out of them. So you give them back before anything horrid happens to you.'

'Are you being rude to us, Shuffle?' said Grabbit. 'Sister, he's being rude. Shall we wish him away to the Land of Dustbins?'

Shuffle was scared. 'Er – is it worthwhile wasting a wish on me, do you think?' he said.

'On the whole, no,' said Grabbit. 'Come on now, Sister, what are we going to wish for? A grand castle set up on that hill over there? My, that would make our friends stare!'

'A grand castle!' snorted Mrs Well-I-Never. 'Just like a man, Grabbit. Who's going to do the work in a great, cold, draughty castle? I'm not going to live there and scrub your floors and cook your dinners, and—'

Mrs Well-I-Never could quite well go on like this

for hours. Grabbit yelled at her.

'All right, all right. We won't have a castle. You think of something.'

'I wouldn't mind a few new hats,' said Mrs Well-I-Never. 'I saw one yesterday with—' Grabbit gave such a loud snort that all the rabbits who were watching darted back to their holes.

'Hats! *Hats!* Just like a woman. What do you want a hat for with a head like yours, and a face like—'

'Mr Tappit's goat,' said little Shuffle, before he could stop himself.

'*Oh!*' said Mrs Well-I-Never, in a rage. 'Well-I-never! Well-I-never-did-in-all-my-life! Grabbit, we must use a wish on Shuffle. We must, we must. What shall we wish? Shall we wish him into an earwig and tread on him? Shall we wish him into a worm and call that fat thrush down? Shall we wish him into a nail in our shoes and walk on him all day long? Shall we—?'

'Hold your tongue,' said Grabbit, impatiently.

'You're full of crazy nonsense. Always have been. I do wish, for once in your life, that you'd be sensible.'

Shuffle gave a squeal of laughter. All the watching rabbits pricked up their ears.

'Now what's so funny?' demanded Grabbit.

'You've wished a wish,' said Shuffle, grinning. 'You wished she'd be sensible for once.'

Mrs Well-I-Never gave a scream. 'Yes, you did! You did! Look at the wishing spells in your hand. One's gone!'

Grabbit looked. Yes, there were only two wishing spells left now. Mrs Well-I-Never grabbed at them and got them.

'There now, you can't waste any more. I've got them both. You be careful, Grabbit. I've got two wishes here, you just be careful.'

Grabbit lost his temper. He ran at his sister and she screamed and ran between the trees. 'Don't shake me! Don't! Oh, Grabbit, I wish you'd go away.'

Shuffle gave another squeal of laughter. Mrs

Well-I-Never looked at him. 'Now what's the matter with you?'

'He's gone. You wished him away,' said Shuffle. 'I say, this is as good as a play. Do go on.'

'Where's he gone?' she said.

'If I knew I wouldn't tell you,' said little Shuffle. 'Good riddance, I say.'

'But – but – he's my brother,' said Mrs Well-I-Never. 'He's not a good brother, but he's the only one I've got. I want him back. Where can I go to look for him?'

'You might try in the Land of Crazy People, or maybe you'd find him in the Land of Grab and Snatch, wherever that is,' said Shuffle, enjoying himself. 'Or possibly in the Land of Rubbish. Or—'

'Don't,' said Mrs Well-I-Never, in tears. 'I didn't mean to wish him away. We shall never see him again. Poor, poor Grabbit.'

'Well, *I* can put up with that all right,' said Shuffle cheerfully. Then he felt sorry for Mrs Well-I-Never.

'Look,' he said, 'have you forgotten the wish that Grabbit wished?'

'Of course I haven't,' said Mrs Well-I-Never. 'A really silly wish – he wished I'd be sensible for once.'

'Well, *be* sensible,' said Shuffle. 'Use your last wish and wish Grabbit back if you want him so badly. But personally I should think a few new hats would be a much better wish for you.'

'Well, I never! To think I didn't think of that!' said Mrs Well-I-Never, cheering up. 'Of course, I've still got a wish left. Grabbit, I wish you back!'

And back he came, frowning and furious. He had been in the Land of Rubbish and it wasn't nice.

Shuffle disappeared, grinning. Well, well, let them argue it out between them. He'd better go back and get three more wishing spells to take to Dame Dandy.

'Ma's right. She said if you gave good things to bad people they would only make bad come out of them,' he said. 'Scoot off, you listening rabbits, the show's over.'

The Girl Who Had Hiccups

The Girl Who
Had Hiccups

There was once a little girl who often got hiccups
when she laughed. I expect you get them sometimes,
don't you? They are funny things to have.

Well, Sheila often had them, and she called them
hee-cups. I don't know if you call them hee-cups, too.
Quite a lot of people do.

Anyway, Sheila was always saying, 'Oh! I've got the
hee-cups again! Mummy, can I have a lump of sugar
to suck?'

That was such a nice cure for the hee-cups. A lump
of sugar is delicious to have in your mouth. First it is
hard and knobbly. Then it goes soft and sweet. Then it

melts altogether and, as Sheila said, you end by drinking it down your throat.

'You *are* lucky to have so many hee-cups, Sheila,' her friends said to her. 'You are always having lumps of sugar to suck!'

Now one day, when Sheila was walking home over Cuckoo Hill, she saw the wind take off the scarecrow's hat nearby, and that made her laugh. She laughed and she laughed.

And then she got hiccups! You know the sort of funny noise you keep making, don't you, when you've got hiccups? You just can't help it. Something seems to catch your breath and you make a noise in your throat.

'I've got the hee-cups!' cried Sheila, as she skipped along over the hill. 'I've got the hee-cups! Oh!'

Then something surprising happened. A small man ran out from behind a tree and went up to Sheila. He had on a blue tunic, and he had pointed ears and slanting green eyes.

'I say! Have you really got some cups?' he asked. 'Where are they? We've just broken ours, and we did so want a picnic.'

Sheila looked down in surprise. 'Are you a brownie, or something?' she asked.

'Yes, of course,' said the little fellow. 'But what about those cups you were shouting about just now?'

'Oh, they were hee-cups I was saying I had got,' said Sheila, with a giggle.

'Well, wouldn't those do to drink from?' said the brownie, pulling at Sheila's hand. 'My friends and I would be so pleased if you would lend them to us. Just for half an hour. Please do. If you will, you can share our picnic.'

Well, Sheila thought it would be marvellous to share in a brownie's picnic. She looked around and saw five more little men peeping out from behind the trees. Some were dressed in blue and some in brown. They all had pointed ears and slanting eyes.

'Listen,' said Sheila. 'I would lend you my hee-cups

if I could – but I can't.'

'Oh, don't be mean,' said the brownie. 'How many have you got?'

'Oh, hundreds I should think!' said Sheila.

'Have they got handles?' asked the brownie.

'Mine haven't,' said Sheila, beginning to giggle again.

'How funny!' said the brownie, puzzled. 'Is there a pretty pattern on them?'

'I shouldn't think so,' said Sheila, and she giggled again. Then she gave a very loud hee-cup. She looked at the little man.

'That was a hee-cup!' she said. 'Didn't you see it? Or did you only hear it?'

'I didn't see anything,' said the brownie. 'I think you are rather an unkind little girl to say you've got such a lot of cups – and yet you won't lend us any. You see, Jinky fell down and broke all ours – and we have some most delicious honey-lemonade to drink.'

'I've never tasted that,' said Sheila, feeling that she

would very much like to. Then a great idea came into her mind. She couldn't give the brownie her hee-cups to put lemonade in, but if they would wait a few minutes she could fetch cups from her dolls' teaset!

'You just wait a minute and I'll fetch you some cups,' she said. And off she sped, running home as fast as ever she could.

She took seven cups. They were white with pink roses round. Back she went to Cuckoo Hill. The six brownies were waiting for her, smiles all over their faces. They had spread a little cloth on the grass and had set out exciting-looking sandwiches and buns. There was a tall jug of honey-lemonade too.

'Oh! She's brought her hee-cups for us after all!' cried the blue brownie, delighted. 'Aren't they pretty?'

Sheila set out the cups. They did look sweet. The brownies really loved them. They poured Sheila a cup of their honey-lemonade at once. She tasted it – and it was simply delicious.

'We do like your little hee-cups,' said the brownies,

pleased. 'They are lovely hee-cups. Have a sandwich?'

Sheila had seven sandwiches and five buns and four cups of honey-lemonade. Then the brownie washed the seven cups in the nearby stream, and gave them back to Sheila.

'Thank you very much,' they said. 'You *are* lucky to have such nice hee-cups!'

Sheila laughed – and her hee-cups came back again. She kept making the kind of noise you have to make when you have hiccups.

'Are you ill or just being rude?' the brownies asked her solemnly. That made Sheila laugh all the more – and her hiccups got much worse. She shouted good-bye and ran home with her little dolls' cups.

'Mummy, I've got hee-cups, please may I have a lump of sugar?' she said. She got her lump of sugar and sucked it, to make the hiccups go.

She put her dolls' cups back into the tea-set box. 'I expect the brownies will always call you hee-cups!' she said.

And they do! You should hear them talking about them.

'We had lemonade in Sheila's hee-cups,' they tell their friends. 'Oh, you should have seen her dear little hee-cups! We're going to buy some for ourselves if we can!'

But they won't be able to, will they?

Christina's Kite

Christina's Kite

When Christina was nine, she had a lovely kite given to her for her birthday. It was a big one, and it had the face of a cat painted on it. Christina was very pleased with it.

'I've never had a kite before,' she said. 'Never! This is a beauty. And oh, what a fine tail it has!'

The kite was red and yellow, and it had a tail of brightly-coloured paper. With it had come a big ball of string.

'And it's a fine windy day too!' said Christina. 'So it will be just right to fly the kite this morning.'

She took it to the hillside, where the wind was very

strong. Alan, Mary, George, and Tom saw her carrying it.

'Many happy returns of the day,' said Mary. 'I say! Is that one of your presents? Can we come and help you to fly it?'

'No,' said Christina, who was very bad at sharing her things with others. 'I want to fly it all by myself. You're not to come with me.'

'You're a selfish girl,' said George. 'You wouldn't let us have a ride on your bicycle the other day, and you wouldn't let us have a try at spinning your top.'

Christina didn't say anything. She turned her back on the others and went on by herself. The others stared after her, and then went on into the fields to play Catch.

Christina unwound a great deal of string. She shook out the kite's tail. She threw it up into the strong wind. It flew high at once. Oh, it was a fine kite pulling strongly at the string, longing to go higher and higher and higher!

'You're a splendid kite!' called Christina joyfully as she watched it climbing into the sky. 'You will soon have used all my string!'

She began to run with the kite, because it pulled so hard – and suddenly she stepped into a rabbit-hole, twisted her ankle, and fell down flat!

'Oh!' cried Christina. 'I've hurt my foot! Oh! I can't get up! Help! Help!'

But the wind blew her voice away, and nobody heard her. The kite pulled hard at the string. Christina was still holding it. The kite was flying high above the field where the other children were playing. How Christina wished she had let them come with her and share the kite! Then they could have helped her.

An idea came into her head. Perhaps the *kite* could help her. She began to pull it in. At last it was lying on the grass beside her. The little girl pulled out her notebook and wrote on a page:

'I have hurt my foot. I am on the hill. Please help me. Christina.'

Then she broke off the last piece of the kite's tail and tied the note there instead. She tried to throw the kite into the air, but it was difficult now she was sitting down. The wind was dropping too – but at last the kite did rise a little, and at once Christina let out some more string.

It flew into the air, but it dipped down and round every now and again because the wind was not so strong now. Still, it flew upwards and was soon high in the air.

And now, when it dipped down, Christina did not pull at the string to make it rise up again. Instead she let the string go slack, so that the kite dipped still further. The wind dropped again – and down went the kite in great circles, dipping right to the ground.

It fell among the children, who were surprised to see it falling there. 'It's Christina's kite,' said Alan.

'We'd better throw it up for her.'

But as they were going to throw it into the wind, Mary noticed the odd bit of white paper tied to the end of the coloured tail.

'Wait a minute,' she said. 'What's this?' She took the note and read it. 'Oh,' she said, 'this is a note from Christina. She's hurt her foot on the hillside. We must go and help her.'

'I don't see why we should,' said George. 'Selfish girl! She won't let us go with her when she's got a new toy – but she wants us quickly enough when she needs help.'

'Don't be mean, George,' said Mary. 'You needn't come if you don't want to – but I shall go, anyhow.'

George went too, and the others. They soon found Christina sitting by the rabbit-hole, her face still white. She couldn't possibly walk on her hurt foot. She had twisted her ankle very badly.

They managed to get her home between them. Her mother was worried when she saw them coming, and ran out to see what was the matter.

'Never mind, Christina,' she said. 'We will put a cold, wet bandage on your ankle, and the swelling will soon go down if you rest it.'

'What about my birthday party?' wept poor Christina.

'Well, dear, as you didn't want anybody to your party except Daddy, Auntie, and me, it won't be much of a disappointment not to have it,' said Mother, who was always feeling sad because Christina wouldn't share things with her friends.

So there was no birthday party for Christina; but later on, when her foot was better, Christina sent out invitation cards to all her friends. She had been thinking a lot whilst she had lain still with her bad ankle.

'I really *am* selfish!' thought Christina. 'I never share anything with anybody – and yet I love to wheel Jenny's pram when she lets me, and I always take one of John's sweets if he offers me any. I feel ashamed of myself now. I wouldn't share my kite – and yet when the other children knew I was hurt they came running to help. I didn't deserve their kindness. But I'll make up for it now.'

So she is having a lovely party now that her foot is better, and is going to share her cake and her chocolates and balloons and toys with everyone. She'll be much happier if she does, won't she?

And *next* time she flies her kite, everyone is going with her to help. They're sure to have a fine time up on the windy hillside.

The Galloping Seahorse

The Galloping Seahorse

Once upon a time a very strange thing happened to Janet. She was having a holiday by the sea, and she was fishing in the rock-pools to see if she could get some shrimps for tea.

She pushed her net along the sand, and then lifted it up to see what she had got in it. There were no shrimps – no little crabs – no fish – but there was something else!

There was a baby mermaid! You know what mermaids are, don't you? – pretty creatures that live in the sea, with heads and arms like those we have, but tails like fishes!

Well, Janet stared at the baby mermaid in her net in great surprise. 'Are you a sea-fairy?' she asked. 'You do look odd with your little fish-tail!'

'I'm a little mermaid!' said the tiny creature in a voice like the splash of a wave. 'I was asleep under a stone, and now you've caught me!'

'I shall show you to my friends,' said Janet, excited.

'No, please don't!' begged the little mermaid. 'I don't want you to. I'm very shy. It is horrid to meet a lot of strange people if you are shy.'

Now it so happened that Janet was shy too, so she knew just how the mermaid felt. It is a horrid feeling to be shy, isn't it?

'Well, if you feel like that, I will put you back in your pool again,' Janet said kindly. That was nice of her, wasn't it? She put her net down into the water carefully, and watched the mermaid swim out of it just like a tiny fish. She disappeared under a stone.

'Well, that was very strange!' said Janet. 'I've never seen a mermaid before.'

Now the next day Janet went to bathe with her friends, and they had a floating rubber bed. It was fun to climb on it and lie down. Janet climbed up too when her turn came, and liked to feel the funny floating bed bobbing up and down on the waves.

The other children began playing with a ball, throwing it to one another. They forgot about Janet and the floating bed. Janet lay flat on her back, looking up into the blue sky. It was lovely.

But do you know, the sea took the bed away, and the wind helped to blow it along – so that when Janet sat up again, she found that she was right out at sea! The beach was ever so far away – and she could hardly hear the shouts of the children playing in the waves with their ball.

Janet was frightened. Suppose she fell off into the deep sea? She could swim a little but not much. She didn't know what to do. It wasn't any good shouting, because she was too far away from the shore for any one to hear.

The little girl looked round her to see if a rowing-boat was near. But no – not a single boat was to be seen. The sea took her farther and farther away as she sat up, wondering what to do.

Janet began to cry. She rubbed her eyes but the tears rolled down her cheeks fast. And then suddenly a funny thing happened!

Just by the bed a tiny head popped up! And whose head do you suppose it was? Can you guess? Yes – it was the head of the little mermaid that Janet had caught in her net the day before. Just think of that!

'What are you crying for?' asked the mermaid, scrambling up on the floating bed.

'Oh, hello, mermaid!' said Janet. 'I'm so pleased to see you. I'm lost on the sea and I don't know what to do.'

'Good gracious!' said the mermaid. 'What a dreadful thing to happen! You should have been more careful. Now, let me see if I can help you. Wait a minute – I must think.'

Janet stared at the tiny creature while she thought hard.

'Can you ride a horse?' the mermaid asked suddenly.

Janet thought that was a very strange thing to ask just then. She nodded her head. 'Yes,' she said. 'I can ride my cousin's pony. I know how to ride. Why?'

'Well, that's all right then,' said the mermaid. 'I can get you one of the white horses we keep here in the sea. You can ride it back to the beach.'

'White horses!' said Janet in surprise. 'What do you mean?'

'Well, haven't you heard people say, when the sea is rather rough, 'Look! There are white horses today'?' asked the mermaid.

'Yes, but I thought they just meant the white curling-over bit of the waves,' said Janet. 'I thought those were the white horses.'

'So they are,' said the mermaid. 'Those white curling pieces are the manes of our white horses. Sometimes they go for a gallop under the sea, and make the sea nice and rough. Their manes just show over the top of the water. Now, I can get you safely back home, but you must never float on the rubber bed again. It's too dangerous; there might not be anyone to help you.'

'What will happen to the floating bed?' asked Janet.

'I'll take care of that,' said the mermaid. 'I and my brothers and sisters will see that the tide takes it to your beach tomorrow, so look for it there. Now I'm just going to get your white horse.'

She dived into the sea. In a minute or two she was back, leading a fine white horse whose curly mane showed just above the water. The horse put its head out and neighed to Janet.

'Slip off the bed on to his back,' said the mermaid. 'He's very gentle. Hold on to his mane when he gallops.'

Janet slid off the bed on to the horse's broad back. 'Goodbye!' called the mermaid from the bed. The horse began to gallop. It was grand fun!

Janet held on to his curly white mane very tightly. Nearer and nearer to the shore they galloped. Janet wanted to shout for joy!

Just as they got into shallow water the horse stopped. Janet slipped off his back and patted his nose. He turned and galloped back. Janet could see his curly mane going farther and farther out to sea.

'Where's the bed – where's the bed?' cried the children, running to Janet. They hadn't seen the horse at all. Janet told them her adventure but they didn't believe her.

'You're a naughty girl, you've lost the bed!' they cried. 'We don't believe your story.'

'The mermaid will bring it back to our beach tomorrow,' said Janet. 'She promised, but she said we shouldn't float on it any more.'

'Well, we'll believe you if we get our bed back,' said the children.

And do you think the floating bed came back? Yes – it did! There it was the next morning, put safely on the sand for the children. So they will have to believe Janet, won't they!

Acknowledgements

All efforts have been made to seek necessary permissions.

The stories in this publication first appeared in the following publications:

'The Fish That Got Away' first appeared in *Sunny Stories*, No. 488, 1950.

'The Enchanted Toadstool' first appeared in *Sunny Stories for Little Folks*, No. 94, 1930.

'Jimmy and the Elephant Man' first appeared in *Enid Blyton's Sunny Stories*, No. 51, 1937.

'The Little Button Elves' first appeared in *Sunny Stories for Little Folks*, No. 102, 1930.

'The Girl Who Was Left Behind' first appeared in *Sunny Stories*, No. 358, 1945.

'A Story of Magic Strawberries' first appeared as 'King Strawberry-Head' in *Teacher's Treasury Vol. 1*, 1926.

'The Marvellous Pink Vase' first appeared in *Enid Blyton's Sunny Stories*, No. 227, 1941.

'When Mollie Missed the Bus' first appeared as 'When Michael Missed the Bus' in *Safety Fun*, No. 3, 1949.

'A Bit of Good Luck' first appeared in *Playways Magazine*, June 1952.

'The Surprising Buns' first appeared in *Sunny Stories*, No. 379, 1946.

'Pretty-Star the Pony' first appeared in *Sunny Stories for Little Folks*, No. 81, 1929.

'The Stolen Shadow' first appeared in *Sunny Stories for Little Folks*, No. 249, 1936.

'On Jimmy's Birthday' first appeared in *Sunny Stories*, No. 531, 1952.

'Bonzo Gets Into Trouble' first appeared in *Sunny Stories for Little Folks*, No. 163, 1933.

'The Roundabout Man' first appeared in *Sunny Stories*, No. 405, 1947.

ACKNOWLEDGEMENTS

'The Fairies' Shoemaker' first appeared as 'Tuppy's Beautiful Sunshade' in *Sunny Stories for Little Folks*, No. 134, 1932.

'Something Funny Going On' first appeared in *Enid Blyton's Magazine*, No. 9, Vol. 5, 1957.

'The Little Toy-Maker' first appeared in *Enid Blyton's Sunny Stories*, No. 239, 1941.

'Billy's Bicycle' first appeared in *Enid Blyton's Sunny Stories*, No. 269, 1942.

'That Girl Next Door!' first appeared in *Sunny Stories*, No. 473, 1950.

'The Boy Who Never Put Things Back' first appeared in *Sunny Stories*, No. 359, 1945.

'Policeman Billy' first appeared in *Sunny Stories for Little Folks*, No. 238, 1936.

'Think Hard, Boatman' first appeared in *Sunny Stories*, No. 418, 1947.

'The Wishing Spells' is untraced, but has appeared in the collection *The Wishing Spells and Other Stories*, 2003.

'The Girl Who Had Hiccups' first appeared in *Enid Blyton's Sunny Stories*, No. 259, 1941.

'Christina's Kite' first appeared in *Enid Blyton's Sunny Stories*, No. 169, 1940.

'The Galloping Seahorse' first appeared in *Enid Blyton's Sunny Stories*, No. 83, 1938.

More classic stories from the world of

Enid Blyton

Enid Blyton's Holiday Stories

A wonderful selection of stories to read and share. From sandcastles at the beach to enchanted ice-creams, step into the summer wit hthese delightful characters. Adventure, fun and magic can all be found on holiday with Enid Blyton, who has been delighting readers for more than seventy years.

More classic stories from the world of

Enid Blyton

The Secret Seven

Join Peter, Janet, Jack, Barbara, Pam, Colin, George
and Scamper as they solve puzzles and mysteries,
foil baddies, and rescue people from danger – all without
help from the grown-ups. Enid Blyton wrote fifteen
stories about the Secret Seven. These editions contain
brilliant illustrations by Tony Ross, plus extra
fun facts and stories to read and share.

More classic stories from the world of

Enid Blyton

The Famous Five Colour Short Stories

Enid Blyton also wrote eight short stories about the Famous Five. Here they are, in their original texts, with brand-new illustrations. They're a perfect introduction to the gang, and an exciting new way to enjoy classic Blyton stories.

Don't miss the first thrilling Secret Stories adventure!

THE SECRET STORIES

The Secret Island

When Peggy, Mike, Nora and Jack find a secret to unravel, their adventures soon begin.

The Arnold children long to run away from their unkind aunt and uncle. But when they escape to a mysterious, deserted island with their friend Jack, they have no idea that an incredible adventure is just beginning …

More classic stories from the world of

Enid Blyton

The Naughtiest Girl

Elizabeth Allen is spoilt and selfish. When she's sent away to boarding school she makes up her mind to be the naughtiest pupil there's ever been! But Elizabeth soon finds out that being bad isn't as simple as it seems. There are ten brilliant books about the Naughtiest Girl to enjoy.